The Wooing of the Bennet Girls

Sequel to '*The Kiss at Lucas Lodge*' - A Pride & Prejudice Variation

By William D. Jamison

CONTENTS

DEDICATION

To my inspiration Jane Austen, A Lady. Without your brilliance there would be no J.A.F.F. community and all of the creation that your works have spurned.

ACKNOWLEDGEMENT

Thank you, Shana Granderson, for being my alpha. To my betas Kimbelle Pease and Carol, I thank you both, you have both improved this story greatly. I appreciate the work of the creatives at Genzi Studio who created the art work for the cover.

FORWARD

This story is the sequel to 'The Kiss at Lucas Lodge'. It is the end of the story, there will be no further sequels.

The story picks up right after the forced wedding of Elizabeth and Darcy with the reluctant bride being carried away from all who she knew and her childhood home.

As the title intimates this sequel is not just about the Darcys, but it tell of how other Bennet girls progress with their romances. We see if Darcy's decision to woo his wife bears any fruit and how the couple move past their wretched beginning.

Even though Wickham met his just ending at the end of the prior book, there is still at least one villain to deal with: Miss Caroline Bingley. We find out is she accepts her banishment to Aunt Hildebrand's with equanimity—*of course not!* We are privy to what she attempts to do about her 'unfair' situation.

We see how the relationship between Thomas and Fanny Bennet grows and if she is able to bring her baby to term. If she does, is it daughter number six or a long desired son?

Enjoy the end of the story that began with a kiss at Lucas Lodge.

CHAPTER 1

Elizabeth was sad when she could no longer see Longbourn as the comfortable Darcy conveyance travelled further and further along the drive of her childhood home. Here she was, sitting in a carriage with her husband, a virtual stranger. How strange that sounded. Her *husband*. She was married to a man that she certainly did not love, did not even like, but at least no longer disliked intensely as she had before the revelations about the now late George Wickham.

Sitting on the forward-facing bench, Elizabeth looked out the window. Now that she could no longer see her former home, she did not really notice anything that passed by. She had some questions for this man she had been forced to marry but was unsure of how to broach them. She had no idea what kind of husband he would be or, more importantly, whether or not he would keep his word about not demanding his marital rights.

"Come, Mr. Darcy, William, we must have some conversation, a very little will do," Elizabeth teased to try and suppress how uncomfortable she felt.

"We may discuss whatever you wish, Elizabeth; I would not suspend any pleasure of yours," he returned.

"I do have a question for you," Elizabeth's now tentative tone concerned him. Seeing his questioning look, seemingly softer than the normal haughty and forbidding visage he had so far been wearing, Elizabeth decided that it was now or never. "You told me that you would not claim your marital rights until I am ready. Do you intend to hold to that and is there a time limit on how long you will wait?" Elizabeth blushed profusely as she asked, but being uncomfortable did not deter her, making it plain that the matter weighed heavily on her mind.

"Do you think that I have so little honour that I would renege on my words as soon as we said, '*I do*?' No, there is no specific date. I would hope at some point you will come to the decision on your own. You do realise that I will need an heir?" Darcy replied, his shoulders falling in obvious dismay. Elizabeth could see that she wounded him by so questioning his honour, though the truth was it was far more than that. She had just given him the first sign of hope and was snatching it back from him. He wanted the same woman he had watched with her family and friends to be with him, and she was again so unsure. He hated that he was the cause when he truly wished her to be happy with him as he knew he could be with her. Neither of them would be happy if she were only a shadow of the woman he had discovered.

"What about my family? Will I be allowed to see them occasionally?" She pointedly ignored his reference to an heir.

"You will not be expected to cut ties with your family. In fact, we will be at Longbourn for Christmas." He informed her.

What her husband had just said caught Elizabeth off guard, and she both wanted to hug him and vent her frustration. Employing the adage that discretion was the better part of valour, she chose to instead give in to neither impulse. "It pleases me that we will spend Christmas with my family, but did you not consider that it may have been a good idea to talk to me about the matter first?" Elizabeth asked more acerbically than was warranted.

"If you wanted to surprise someone with something that you believed would make them happy, would you talk to them ahead of time?" Darcy asked directly. '*Is this how it is to be? Will she always look for the worst in me? I suppose I have earned her disdain; I did force her into this marriage.*'

Elizabeth felt as though she had been hoisted on her own

petard. She was looking for something that was not there, and all he was trying to do was give her pleasure. If she were honest with herself, she knew that there were many places that he could have preferred to be for Christmas. Yet, he had done what she would want! Could she truly accuse him of having selfish disdain for the feelings of others when she was presented with such clear and convincing evidence to the contrary?

"I apologise, William," she offered softly. "I suppose that it will take a while to get used to one another."

"You have the right of it. We said that we would start again, yet I wonder how we are to do that if you look for the worst motives in anything that I do." he pointed out.

"It may take me some time, but I will try to change the way I see things," Elizabeth conceded. "May I ask you an honest question?" It may be a hard question for you to hear," she warned when Darcy nodded his acquiescence.

"Please ask whatever you want answered so that we may, in fact, go forward," Darcy replied.

"You and Georgiana have both told me of how Wickham would take what he wanted regardless of the feelings of the other party, correct?" She asked carefully and Darcy nodded in agreement. "Tell me how your forcing my hand and compromising me was not the same as what he has done?"

His first reaction *was* anger at hearing her compare him to such a wastrel as *Wickham*! He was *nothing* like the soon to be executed rapist! But given the fact that she had warned him he would not like her question, he forced himself to replay her exact words again in his mind. He was glad he had not reacted as he initially was inclined. She had just done so, and he had been hurt at her ascribing the worst to him. This was a pattern they would need to break, and he was glad to be the first to try to. She was not *saying* he was the same; she was *asking* a legitimate question.

Elizabeth watched the emotions play over her husband's

face. When she saw the thunderous expression that played on his face, she was afraid that she had pushed too hard but was relieved when she saw him relax somewhat. She had noticed before that William did not ever give a flippant or glib answer; he almost always would consider his words carefully and seemed to be doing so now. She waited patiently, already knowing that it was best not to talk until he was ready to answer her.

It took Darcy a little longer than five minutes to formulate his answer. "I will allow that there is something in common, as you were forced. However, you were not forced in the same way nor with the same intentions. I have apologised for stealing your choice from you, and I will keep doing so until you accept that I am sincere."

"William, I..." Elizabeth was stayed by her husband's hand on her arm, his touch sudden when he leaned forward and closed the physical distance between them somewhat, though the metaphorical distance was far greater than she knew how to measure.

"Elizabeth, please, allow me to speak. When I have said what I feel I need to, you may comment and ask as many questions as you feel you need to. Is that acceptable to you?" Darcy asked. Relieved, Elizabeth nodded. "Wickham always planned his seductions, used manipulation and lies to gain an upper hand, and his aim was one of two things, or both in Georgiana's case.

"His intention was almost always to take the virtue of a young lady and to find a way to gain wealth that he did not have to earn. His *modus operandi* was to *promise* marriage in an attempt to get her submission, but without a fortune like our sister's, he would move on as soon as he got that which he desired. He had no care for their broken hearts or if he left them behind in delicate condition. He would move on, likely having already chosen his next victim.

"Now, let us turn to my case. It was not planned; I did not

abandon you to fend for yourself with your reputation in tatters, and there was no financial incentive for me." Darcy saw the look that Elizabeth gave him. "You may not want to hear that, but we both know it is the truth."

"It is. Please continue, William," Elizabeth allowed quietly. She had asked him to face something uncomfortable, it was only fair that she do the same.

"Not only did I not abandon you, but I also proposed marriage and followed through with the intent. Unlike Wickham, I returned to you as soon as I was able. And before you say it, yes, it would have been better for you had I walked away at Lucas Lodge and not kissed you. It also would have been better for me as you would not be so mistrustful or angry with me. However, as we are both intelligent people, we know there is nothing either of us can do to change the past. What I hope is that we do not allow the past to determine our future together, though it will inevitably shape it." William said in summation.

It was Elizabeth's turn to consider all his words. If she were honest, her husband was correct. The only similarity, and it was tenuous at best, was the compromise of a public kiss. He never attempted to seduce her and was always a consummate gentleman, aside from the insult at the assembly for which she had forgiven him.

When she looked at what he said objectively and not with the intent of trying to find fault with him, she had to own that all he had said rang true. Could she have asked the same question without inferring a comparison to the man that she now knew was a libertine? The truthful answer was that she, of course, could have.

Why was it that she was still trying to wound him at every turn even though she had agreed to begin again? Evidently, her husband was not the only one capable of implacable resentment. When she looked at herself in that light, Elizabeth was ashamed of her own hypocrisy. Was she not the one who espoused to only look at the past as the remembrance gave you pleasure? It seemed to her that she needed to start to follow some of her own advice. Discovering herself to be a hypocrite was not a revelation that Elizabeth enjoyed.

"I thank you for your well-reasoned explanation, William, and I agree that there is no comparison between the two of you. I will never infer that is the case again; you have my word," Elizabeth offered peace and contrition.

"As much as I hate to hear myself and *that* individual mentioned in the same breath, I do understand the genesis of your question. I did, after all, steal your right to choose your mate in life, and now we are bound together, for better or worse, for our lifetimes. I pledge to you here and now that I will honour our vows. I will *never* be with another for the rest of my life, regardless of how long it takes you to decide to consummate our marriage," Darcy promised, his sincerity absolute.

He had just answered another of the questions Elizabeth had wanted to ask but had not known how to phrase. "You have saved me the mortification of trying to discover your intentions on that subject, William, so I thank you. There is but one part of the vows that I am not able to perform today, which is the one regarding love. As to the rest, like you I will adhere to them completely," Elizabeth offered a small smile.

"I will not delude myself that you will wake up on the morrow and be in love with me. My sincerest hope is that as you come to know the real me, and not the man I present in public to keep the fortune huntresses away, you will at the very least come to like me, and, if nothing else, we will become friends," Darcy stated openly.

"There are far worse options than to be friends with the person you are married to," she agreed, unwilling to voice the fact that there were also other options she had wished for when she was married. That was all lost to her, so there was no point in hurting both of them by saying that she had hoped to love her husband before they were married.

'Yes, mayhap we will become friends. I am starting to see that there is a lot more to my husband than I had assumed. It is incumbent on me to try and look for the positive in him,' Elizabeth told herself.

From that point on the newlyweds did not talk, and it was not too long later that the silence became a companionable one.

--*-*-*-*-*-*-*-*-*-*-*

Thomas Bennet summoned his family, including William Collins, to the drawing room after he and Lydia had returned from Colonel Forster's office. Once they were all seated, he paced for a few seconds as he decided how to break the news that Colonel Fitzwilliam had shared with him before his departure back to his unit.

"There is no easy way to tell any of you this, so I will just tell you. Both Wickham and Denny will be executed at dawn on the morrow for rape and other crimes," Bennet informed his family. For a few blissful seconds there was silence, then gasps and exclamations filled the room.

"In the end, everything that Lizzy, Mr. Darcy, and Colonel Forster had said about Wickham was true, was it not, Papa?" Lydia asked calmly, which was so far from what he expected, he went close in case she needed him.

"Yes, Lydia, it was all true. He confessed to his interrogators that he wanted to ruin you as a way to get back at us for banning him from Longbourn as well as exposing his predilection for ruining young girls and leaving debts behind wherever he went. Your new brother owns a few thousands in the blackguard's vowels and has helped a number of families that had been left with ruined daughters who were with child," Bennet related, understanding the sharp gasps from his womenfolk.

"Papa, why did our new brother do all that? I cannot imagine it was just a sense of Christian duty, though I am sure that was some of it." Mary asked. She was confused, for she had long believed that the world was all black or white but lately she had started to see that the world was instead coloured with shades of grey.

"My new son is a complicated man, Mary. He is, however, a most honourable one. I accept that his compromise of Lizzy was unplanned, that it was a moment in which he let his vaunted control slip because he was already in need of her joy and happiness as he has had little in his life since his mother passed. He has cleaned up after Wickham, but not out of any sense of camaraderie for the wastrel; William has no such feelings for that man. He felt that it was his duty because of his father's appreciation of Wickham, regardless of how misplaced it was. It was his father that gifted the man a gentleman's education. William believes that his father's actions led to some of the unrealistic expectations that Wickham had, so he felt it was his duty as his father's son to clean up after Wickham's destruction," Bennet explained.

"It seems that I have to learn to start looking at things from many different angles," Mary said introspectively.

"If you ever need to talk, Cousin Mary, I am a good listener," Collins volunteered.

Mary blushed lightly. Normally, no one noticed her, yet Mr. Collins was going beyond that and offering to talk to her if she felt the need. Mary felt a stirring in her stomach that she could not immediately identify. "Thank you for your generous offer, Mr. Collins; I will remember that." The warm sensation started to deepen, and she realised that this, this excitement, this feeling with the hope that he would continue to notice her meant that she was inclined toward him.

It was as Jane and Elizabeth promised it would be, this first inclination, but she really would have liked to have been prepared for the racing of her heart. As she watched him, she considered that he had gone against a woman's wishes to the betterment of his parish and her racing heart swelled as feelings of awe, admiration, and attraction intensified. Everything froze when someone took her hand and she looked up, her shock increasing to discover it was Lydia.

"He would be lucky to win you." Lydia whispered softly and held her hand tighter, saying nothing else and helping Mary catch her breath.

Bennet had expected much caterwauling when he had made his announcement, so he was beyond surprised at the restrained reaction from his youngest. He knew that she had been shocked when they had gone to meet with the Colonel, but he expected that she would put that out of her mind as an inconvenient fact. He looked to his wife, and she nodded, knowing what he was about to announce next would be hard for them all, but this gesture gave him hope as maybe nothing had before.

"Lydia, your mother and I have decided that you are to go to school. *We* made the mistake of allowing you and your sisters into society before you were prepared, and now we must correct *our* errors. Our lack of proper care of you and your sisters could have led to your ruin and that of your sisters. As you now know, both you and Kitty are back in until you are at least eight and ten. You will be going to the Wrightfield School for Young Ladies in Wiltshire." Bennet was sure that this news would cause a tantrum. He was not prepared for the almost stoic response.

"When do I leave, Papa?" Lydia asked calmly.

"After Twelfth Night. I will accompany you to your school. If you do well in your first year, we will seek a school closer to Hertfordshire. Kitty," Bennet turned to his second youngest daughter, "you will go the same school as your new sister Georgiana which concentrates on music and on your talents of drawing and painting. Mary, you may either go to the same school to study music, or we are willing to hire a music master for you."

"From the little time that I have spent with our new sister, I am happy that she will be at the same school," Kitty smiled. Not only would she be out from under Lydia's shadow, but she would study subjects that were close to her heart.

"Papa, if it is all the same to you, I would prefer a music master here. I am almost nine and ten, and I am sure that I will be older than all of the other girls at the school," Mary reasoned.

"Then it will be so, Mary," Bennet allowed.

"No school for me, Papa?" Jane asked in jest.

"You, daughter, are being courted, so no, we are not sending you anywhere," Mrs. Bennet stated, not catching the jest.

"No, Jane, we are not sending you away to school," Bennet focused on his eldest daughter. He was ashamed of the retort that he almost made; his first inclination was to make sport of his wife, but he would no longer behave in such a way towards his Fanny. "Your mother is right in that you are being courted, but more importantly you are a model of decorum and gentleness anyone could emulate and be better for it."

"I am feeling fatigued, Jane dearest. Will you assist me up to my chambers?" Mrs. Bennet requested. Jane stood and offered her arm to her mother as they departed the drawing room.

'I am concerned for Fanny; she has not been fatigued like this... since she was with CHILD! Could it be? We will have to ask Mr. Jones to examine her,' Bennet thought to himself anxiously. He would make his request quickly, as he could not imagine his life without her, though he was struck dumb at the possibility that he would be a father one more time. 'I suppose six daughters are better that five!' he told himself, not allowing himself to consider having a son after so many disappointments in that area. Another daughter that could blend all his daughters, be a perfect replica of his wife, or be another Lizzy who would be a true pleasure to have running around.

--*-*-*-*-*-*-*-*-*-*-*-*-*

Miss Caroline Bingley was fuming. She had arrived at her Aunt Hildebrand's house an hour previously, and already she wanted to kill the woman. There would be no society, no fashion, and worst of all no allowance! *Her* money would go to the old biddy rather than to her!

If she were to escape from this nightmare of a place in the wilds of Yorkshire, then she would need to relieve her aunt of some funds. It would not be stealing when she was only taking back her own money, after all. She had found a way to take money from Charles; she would find a way to do so here as well.

Unfortunately for Miss Bingley, Miss Hildebrand Bingley, her late father's spinster sister, was not approaching her dotage but was a spry and very much aware woman of three and fifty. She had loved one man many years ago, but he had chosen connections and wealth over love. Hildebrand had decided then that she would not marry. It gave her no solace that the man had himself had a short and miserable marriage. He drank himself to death before he and his wife had had their ten-year anniversary.

"Caroline, a letter just arrived for you from your brother," Aunt Hildebrand informed her niece.

Miss Bingley lit up. She was sure that the missive was one apologising to her and begging her to return to his house, so she broke the seal with gusto.

14 October 1811

Netherfield, Hertfordshire

You failed, Caroline. Lady Catherine and all of Darcy's family, yes, the Earl and Countess included, approve of Miss Elizabeth, Mrs. Darcy by the time this reaches you.

Your letter did nothing except bring Lady Catherine and her daughter, Miss de Bourgh, to witness the wedding for themselves.

I am disgusted by your machinations, vitriol, lying, and spite. Consider this my final letter to you.

CB

"**No**! This cannot be!" Miss Bingley yelled as she ripped the offending missive into as many pieces as she was able and cast it on the ground.

"Pick that up!" Aunt Hildebrand ordered. She was almost amused at the pinched look on her niece's mien. "If you make a mess wilfully as you just did, you and *not one* of my servants will clean it." As Miss Bingley turned to storm out of the room, he aunt halted her. "The paper will remain here until you remove it, and you will be locked in your chamber with no food until you do!"

The following morning the fuming woman, swearing revenge on everyone, was hungry enough to clean up her own mess.

CHAPTER 2

Mrs. Elizabeth Darcy was in a state of shock. She had known that her husband was rich, but when they pulled up to the Grosvenor Square town house, which she herself would term a mansion, she had not been prepared for the imposing edifice that she spied when her husband had said that they were traveling to their house in town. There was a couple standing on the top step just outside the open front door.

Darcy saw the direction of his wife's gaze. "My, no, our butler and housekeeper, Mavis and Amos Payton. They have served the Darcy family since before my dear mother left this world," Darcy informed his wife.

Darcy stepped out of the coach and handed his wife out. While she had extended her hand to him, she had also made sure that there was as little physical contact as possible. Due to the cold temperature, no one lingered outside so it was unnoticed by any except Darcy.

If she had been in awe when she saw the façade of Darcy House, it was nothing to what Elizabeth felt when she stood in the entrance hall as the butler and a footman divested them of their outerwear. Given the circumstances of her marriage, Elizabeth had refused to consider the purchase of a trousseau. As she surveyed her surroundings and saw the looks of some of the servants when seeing her mode of dress, she acknowledged that her refusal had been short-sighted.

Darcy opened the door to a drawing room and informed her it was the yellow drawing room. Elizabeth walked inside briefly. It was not as she thought it would be. After she exited the drawing room, Darcy pointed out where the master's study was and its counterpart next door for the mistress.

The thing that surprised Elizabeth more than any other was the lack of gaudy and ostentatious decoration. She had assumed that his house would be decorated in a manner similar to Rosings that Cousin William had told them about, or to Caroline Bingley's taste. He had not spared his opinion of the distasteful way that Rosings had been decorated. As she remembered her cousin's narrative, Elizabeth had a feeling that after Anne and Richard married there would be many changes made to that estate.

Darcy offered Elizabeth his arm and she placed her hand on it lightly as he led her up to the master suite. He then stopped in front of three doors. "To the right are my chambers, the centre door is our shared sitting room, and your chambers are to the left. Would you like me to give you a quick tour of the master apartments?" Darcy asked.

"That would be nice, thank you, William," Elizabeth answered with a little more warmth in her tone than had so far been there when talking specifically to Darcy.

Darcy opened the centre door and indicated that she should go ahead of him. "Our sitting room," he stepped aside so she could survey the room unimpeded. It looked like an extremely comfortable room and, surprisingly, it seemed to have been designed for comfort. As she had seen so far in the house, everything was of the highest quality, and had a tone of understated elegance.

There were two sofas, two arm chairs that looked rather inviting, a bookcase filled with tomes, a sideboard, and a low table between the two sofas. Elizabeth noticed a small table with two chairs near the big windows which had a window seat. She guessed this was where Darcy had eaten many a meal when alone in the big house. Elizabeth could visualise herself with her feet curled up below her, sitting in that very window seat with a volume of poetry or prose in her hand.

Next, Darcy opened the door that led to the master's chambers. Elizabeth did not feel comfortable entering his domain, so she gave a quick look from the doorway. The room was decorated for a man, in tones of green and brown. She did not miss that it also included the biggest bed that she had ever seen. She made a quick turn away from his room and Darcy closed the door, leading her to the opposite door, which led into her new chambers.

Elizabeth walked in ahead of her husband and found a maid waiting for them. "This is Upton, your lady's maid. Mrs. Payton assigned one for you as you do not have your own as yet. If you are not happy with the housekeeper's choice, you are free to hire a maid of your own choosing," Darcy informed Elizabeth.

To Elizabeth it seemed like an unnecessary extravagance, but she chided herself with the reminder that she should become accustomed to her new station in life. She had almost accused him of being officious, and immediately felt ashamed that she again had been quick to presume the worst possible explanation. Thankfully, she had avoided accusing him of ignoring her in the choice of her personal servant before he offered her the explanation.

'I have to stop doing that!' Elizabeth remonstrated herself.

"If you would like to wash or bathe and then change, dinner will be in an hour. Also, please feel free to redecorate anything to reflect your preferences, especially your chambers. They have not been updated for nigh on thirty years, when my mother was a new bride at Darcy House," Darcy told her before he turned and left her alone with the maid.

Her chambers were larger than all her sisters' chambers at Longbourn combined. She could understand why Miss Bingley coveted this place given that her chambers made those at Netherfield look small, and she had considered them large. It was true that the décor was not what Elizabeth would have chosen for herself. Pinks, peaches, and light violets were not colours that Elizabeth preferred, so she would indeed redecorate her chambers. If her husband would allow it, she would invite Aunt Madeline to come view the room, as she was one of the best decorators Elizabeth could name and her style matched what she had so far seen of the house perfectly.

As for the rest of the house, nothing she had so far seen required a change to match her own tastes, but she would reserve judgement until her tour of the whole house, hopefully with her aunt to aid her. She had never been one to do as some would by making changes just because there was money allotted for the option; she would only want to update something if it was necessary.

*_*_*_*_*_*_*_*_*_*_*_*_*_*

As there had been a fair amount of food remaining from the wedding breakfast, Mrs. Bennet sent a note to Netherfield Park inviting Bingley and the Hursts for a family dinner. With the house now empty, as Darcy's family had returned to London after the wedding breakfast, there would be only three additional dinner guests. Mrs. Hurst responded with a grateful affirmative.

Bingley was impatient to see Jane again. They had not been courting for long, but he was hoping to see some sign of her acceptance of him so that he could propose to her. He was sure that she was the one for him, the only one. While it was true he had been infatuated with a few women before Jane, he could now tell that he had never been in love with any other. He now realised the others were but mild flirtations compared to what he was feeling. He was truly and irrevocably in love with Jane Bennet.

Bingley would have proposed already, but for the concern of pressing his suit when she might not be ready. With Darcy's compromise of Miss Bennet's sister so recent, he wanted to be sure that she was ready to take the step without undue pressure. There had been a time that he believed her mother would have pushed her to accept his proposals regardless of her feelings, but the changes in Mrs. Bennet's behaviour since her daughter's sojourn at Netherfield had been marked, which thankfully meant that should Jane say yes, it would be because she wanted to of her own accord.

Bingley had been in company with his angel enough to tell the difference in the way that she smiled and looked at him and the way that she looked at others. Yes, she smiled at others, but the deeper warmth and pleasure in her eyes was for him alone. This observation led him to the conclusion that even if his Jane were not in love with him yet, she would be soon, and he could wait. He would wait as long as necessary.

The Bingley carriage arrived at Longbourn at exactly five in the afternoon, and the three were welcomed into the Bennet's drawing room. On greeting one another Bingley noticed that only three of the Miss Bennets, their father, and their cousin were present. Jane smiled at his questioning look.

"Lydia is feeling somewhat indisposed and decided to take her meal above stairs this evening, and Mama is resting," Jane informed the guests.

Bennet was sitting with Collins, and Hurst chose to join their conversation. It had not gone unnoticed that once Miss Bingley had been sent away, Mr. Hurst no longer over imbibed or slept when not eating or drinking. Miss Bingley's absence had been a boon to everyone, and none could quite make themselves repine it.

Mrs. Hurst sat with Mary and Kitty. "Is your mother well?" she asked out of concern.

"Mama was feeling a little fatigued after the wedding and celebratory meal. She went to rest and should be down soon to join us for dinner," Mary informed her guest.

"I wonder how Lizzy is doing in London," Jane asked Bingley with concern.

"I am confident that she will be well, Miss Bennet," Bingley soothed her. "What Darcy did was out of character, but he is honourable and will make sure that your sister is treated as she should be."

"To tell you the truth, I worry more about how Lizzy will treat Mr. Darcy. She can be very obstinate and slow to forgive. At least she knows that most of her opinions about the man were not true and all had been formed from his slighting her at the assembly," Jane opined.

"His outburst at the assembly was because I would not leave him alone when I knew that he was in no mood to dance. His choices were to either come to the assembly or to remain at Netherfield with my younger sister. You can understand why he chose the assembly," Bingley owned. "Let us not canvass the past. How are you doing, Miss Bennet? I know you and Mrs. Darcy are the closest of sisters; I am sure that you will miss her terribly."

"I am quite well, Mr. Bingley," Jane replied. "Yes, Lizzy and I are more than sisters; we are the best of friends and I miss her already. We used to talk every night before bed for as long as I am able to remember, so it will be very strange not to have her here tonight. What a selfish creature I am, thinking of myself when Lizzy is on her own in a new home!"

"You, Miss Bennet, are the least selfish person I know," Bingley stated with meaning as he lifted one of Jane's hand and bestowed a kiss on it, forgetting that they were not alone. "It is my hope that you will soon have another to confide in." Both blushed profusely when Bennet cleared his throat. The blushes deepened when giggles from the three females on the settee were heard.

"What is so amusing?" A refreshed Fanny Bennet asked as she walked in and took her seat in the drawing room.

"Nothing in particular, my dear. Our daughter's suitor forgot that he was not alone," Bennet informed his wife with a knowing smile.

Jane and Bingley were rescued from further sport at their expense when Mr. Hill announced that dinner was served. Bennet waited until the younger people stood and were on their way to the dining parlour and then approached his wife to escort her. "I think we need to have either Mr. Jones or the midwife examine you, Fanny, my dearest wife," he told Mrs. Bennet in a whisper.

"That would be a good idea, Thomas. I believe we both suspect the same thing. Oh, Thomas, what if it is another daughter?" Mrs. Bennet fretted.

"Then we will love her as we love all of her sisters," Bennet responded, giving his wife a comforting kiss on the cheek.

--*-*-*-*-*-*-*-*-*-*-*-*

"Do you think our nephew will be able to win over his wife?" Lady Catherine asked her brother and sister.

"Win her over!" scoffed Ulysses Fitzwilliam, Viscount Smithtown. "A country nobody should be falling over herself to please one as high as our cousin Darcy."

"I could not agree more," his wife Lady Jaqueline added spitefully.

"Are you two addlepated?" The Earl growled at them both. Lord Reginald Matlock had no idea how his older son had become so snobbish and disdainful of others. He and Richard had grown up in the same house and yet were vastly different in character. "How many times have you been told who compromised who, and that our niece, your *cousin*, did not desire a marriage to William!"

"I-I was only jesting, father," the Viscount stammered. He did not want to anger his father and have his allowance reduced once again. His habits had already been restricted. His father had refused to cover his overspending and his debts of honour. He had frittered away almost all his wife's dowry at the tables, and he often wished that the Earl would up and die so he would control all of the Matlock fortune, but the old man was, unfortunately, the picture of health. Ulysses Fitzwilliam led a dissipated lifestyle but harming or having others cause his father harm would be beyond the pale, even for him.

"Before my son and daughter-in-law interrupted us," Lady Elaine gave both a look of censure, "I was about to say that William will have to work extremely hard to win her approbation. In the little time that I spoke to Elizabeth before the wedding, I could tell that she cares naught for wealth and position in society, so those attributes will not help William. She has an independent streak in her that our nephew will run afoul of if he tries to order her life without consulting her beforehand."

Anne de Bourgh, who had needed a long rest after the exertion of attending the festivities of the morning and the journey to London after, entered the drawing room with her companion. "Were you talking about my new Cousin Lizzy, Aunt Elaine?" Anne asked.

"We were," Lady Elaine responded with warmth. She was overjoyed that Richard was, at that very moment, at his general's office resigning his commission and putting it up for sale. Richard would not be sent into harm's way again!

"Where is my betrothed?" Anne asked innocently, aware that her older cousin and his wife, who she had no time for, were not aware of her impending nuptials to Richard.

"Who are you betrothed to, Anne? Darcy is married already, is he not?" came the Viscount's snarky comment.

"You are very familiar with my betrothed; he is your brother, after all." Anne's saccharine sweet answer came with a matching smile.

"Richard! You are to marry Richard?" the shocked Viscount spluttered. He had always lorded over his brother because he was naught but a poor second son. Now he would no longer be poor and would be the master of a large and very profitable estate long before Ulysses inherited Matlock, with a hefty fortune to boot!

"Yes, your brother, Richard." Anne confirmed calmly.

"Aunt Catherine, I thought that you always wanted to combine Rosings and Pemberley!" He tried again to find a way out of this humiliation.

"Neither Anne nor Darcy desired the same," Lady Catherine informed her nephew. She herself used to think more like the Viscount and had only changed her perspective within the last forty-eight hours. Now that she could see how his supercilious behaviour was perceived by others, she felt even more shame for the way she used to behave. "Besides, that would not be possible, even had they desired it, as your cousin was married this very morning!" The Viscount and Viscountess, to the pleasure of all in the drawing room, decided to depart.

"Cathy, we will have to help introduce Lizzy to society. I am sure that she needs a new wardrobe, so let us take her so the *ton* will see that she has our full support and approbation," Lady Elaine suggested.

"That is a grand idea, Elaine. It is so good to be welcomed back into the bosom of my family rather than having to hide away at Rosings like it is my personal fiefdom," Lady Catherine replied sadly as she thought about all the time she lost with her family because her behaviour had pushed them away.

"I, we, are very happy to have my sister back, Cat," Lord Reginald promised. "I always hoped that I would see this day. It is a pity that Anne and George are no longer with us to see us all as a family once again."

"We know that the Darcys are not having a traditional honeymoon, so what say you that we call on them on the morrow, sister?" Lady Elaine asked.

"That is a good idea, Elaine. What about your daughter-in-law? Will she be trouble with regards to the new Mrs. Darcy?" Lady Catherine wondered, then quickly turned to the more important matter first, which was to allow her daughter a choice rather than presume she knew her answer. "Anne, would you like to join us for a shopping expedition with Elizabeth?"

"I would, Mama. And before you ask, as long as I am able to sit at the various shops, I will be well," Anne responded, her pleasure at being so considered obvious. Lady Catherine winced inwardly, wondering how she had ever believed her daughter smiled during these last years now that she saw her genuine smiles.

"We will have to take the Viscountess with us, whether she wants to or not," Lady Elaine decided. "If she then says anything bad about Elizabeth, she will look like a bigger fool than she is thought to be by society."

"What are we to do with our son and daughter-in-law? You know that some day soon they will drag the House of Matlock through the mud. Our son's penchant for married women will not end well, and given what we know of his wife's infidelities, how could we know if any child she bears a will be legitimate?" Lord Reginald mused.

"Mayhap this is a discussion that we should have when my maiden daughter is not present," Lady Catherine objected.

"Mother, I have heard the whispers, and I am not as clueless as you think," Anne replied with some impertinence.

"It seems that your new cousin is rubbing off on you, Anne. I look forward to getting to know you both better," Lady Elaine smiled.

--*-*-*-*-*-*-*-*-*-*-*-*

The following morning Captain Carter came to see Mr. Bennet and was shown into the master's study. "The sentence has been carried out," the Captain informed Mr. Bennet. "Neither Wickham nor Denny will harm a young lady again."

"Please convey my thanks to Colonel Forster for sending you to inform me. We can only pray that the blacksmith's daughters do not become with child," Bennet responded.

The Captain agreed and bade Bennet a farewell. Bennet walked him to the door just in time to welcome Mr. Jones to the house. "We suspect that my wife may be with child again, Jones." Bennet shared.

"Let me examine her and we will see," Mr. Jones chuckled as Bennet escorted the apothecary up the stairs to the shared bedchamber.

It was less than ten minutes when Mr. Jones returned to the hall. "Your wife would like to see you, Bennet," Mr. Jones grinned at the expectant man.

"Thomas, it is confirmed! I am with child. Whoever would have thought that fifteen years after Lydia, I would be in this state again?" Fanny laughed ruefully. "How can this be?"

"You know how it happened, Fanny! We were both there. It is good news, Fanny, and as I said, whatever we have, as long as both mother and babe are healthy, it will be a blessing from God above," Bennet laughed with her.

"Are you in agreement that I wait for the quickening to inform our family?" Fanny asked.

"Yes, my love, I agree whole heartedly as I have five times in the past. I am rather surprised you asked at all as you well knew the answer," Bennet drawled, winking at her to again hear her laugh. "Did Jones give you an estimate of when our blessing will arrive?"

"It should be in May or June of next year, so I should feel the quickening somewhere around Twelfth Night," Fanny offered.

Bennet informed his wife of what the Captain had told him, and after what the one miscreant had attempted to do to two of her daughters, Fanny had no sympathy for the men. Bennet kissed his wife soundly and returned to his study to give her time to dress.

CHAPTER 3

The previous night Elizabeth Darcy had had a long conversation with herself. She promised herself that she would not look for the worst possible motives in anything that her husband did or said. She also realised that assumptions and suppositions were counterproductive and would only lead to misunderstandings.

She resolved to talk to her husband at the first possible opportunity and truly start over in deed, and not just with words. She admitted to herself that her resentment over the compromise had led her to suggest a new start by means of appearing to accept the situation, but her heart had not been in it.

Since the compromise, her husband had been nothing but solicitous of her feelings, so it was incumbent on her to also try. The members of his family, or at least the ones that she had met, had been accepting of her even as they censured William for his actions. She liked them all and they seemed to like her, and to everyone's surprise that included Lady Catherine de Bourgh. That great lady had pledged herself to change, so Elizabeth Darcy could do so as well.

Upton helped her mistress dress and gave her directions to the breakfast parlour. That had proved unnecessary, as her husband was patiently waiting in the hall and offered her an arm to guide her downstairs. Rather than barely touch his arm as she had yesterday, she wound her hand around his arm, causing him to arch his brow. Whether in question of her motivations or concern for her well-being she was not certain, though she had to admit it was likely both.

"Did you sleep well, Elizabeth?" Darcy asked gently.

"Yes, William, I truly did. That is the most comfortable mattress I have ever slept on. I had suspected that I would not sleep well without sharing a bed with Jane, but I was asleep almost as soon as my head was on the pillow," Elizabeth offered him a careful smile as she gave him the particulars.

Darcy was heartened by the changes he was seeing this morning. While he did not believe that a fairy had waved a magic wand, causing Elizabeth to fall madly in love with him, what he did see was that she was trying. The realisation induced waves of relief and cautious hope which washed over him as he guessed that now that she was fully unable to go backward, she had, at last, truly allowed herself to begin again.

Darcy led Elizabeth into a nice sized parlour where she spied a sideboard with what looked like enough food to feed a small army rather than just the two of them. "This is the small dining parlour, Elizabeth. We use it for breaking our fasts and meals at which less than eight people are expected," Darcy explained.

"If this is the small parlour, I hesitate to think what the large one is like," Elizabeth returned, her brow arched with playful challenge.

"May I make you a plate, Elizabeth?" Darcy asked, relieved when his wife nodded her agreement. Darcy had paid attention to her preferences at Netherfield and surprised her by selecting the items that she would have for herself.

After a footman poured tea for her and coffee for him, the newlyweds were left alone, and the doors closed. "William, I have something to tell you, but first I need to ask your permission for something," Elizabeth opened the conversation.

"I hope that you will never fail to ask me anything when you feel the need," Darcy nodded to indicate that he was ready for her question.

"You remember that you met my Aunt and Uncle Gardiner at the wedding?" Darcy again nodded. "May I invite them to Darcy House? I know with my uncle being actively engaged in trade..." Elizabeth stopped her question as Darcy raised his hand.

"It will not be my habit to cut you off when you speak, Elizabeth, but I want to make sure that you understand what I am about to tell so that there will be no misunderstanding today or any of our future days. You, and you alone, are mistress of all our houses, *including* this one! It is your prerogative to invite *whoever* you choose to. As it so happens, I found the Gardiners both intelligent and gentle and I would enjoy getting to know them better," Darcy pressed his point. "All I ask is that you notify me who you are inviting, and if there is anyone that I object to, I will inform you. You will be told why, and then you will be free to make your decision. In some cases it will be for reasons not having to do with the request to invite, only that we have engagements elsewhere, or that I have promised to do something when you might expect me here, such as visit with my solicitors at their office."

Elizabeth was silent for a minute as she digested the whole of what he had said. This certainly was not the man she had expected to be married to, and she knew that she had made the right decision to try. It was harder to ignore her conscience telling her that she could have learned that sooner. She did not know if she would ever love her husband, but for the first time she could honestly see them becoming friends. In her mind, she had moved on from just merely tolerating him to genuinely wanting to get to know him.

"I owe you an apology, William." Elizabeth saw that her husband was about to object and raised a hand to stop him from doing so. "Please wait until I have completed what I would like to say, William." Darcy nodded. "I told you before our wedding that I agreed to start again, but that is not what I did. I was still assuming the worst and refused to see that not only are you an honourable man, but you are a good one as well. You have my word of honour that from now on I will look for the positive, not the negative.

"What I would like to propose is that if either of us does not understand the meaning of something the other says or does that we do not assume the intents and thoughts behind them. There have been too many misunderstandings. I pledge to ask you, to talk to you before I presume intentions, good or bad, so that I can understand you, even if I do not like the situation." Elizabeth was not normally built for sadness, but she had allowed herself to become maudlin over things she could not change. Unless she changed some of her attitudes, she would have a sad existence by her own hand.

"I do not want to talk over you, so I want to verify that you have said what you wanted to say?" Darcy asked when there had been a little time with silence.

"Perhaps we need a signal for that? Like two nods or a slight wave? At least until we are more in tune with one another?" Elizabeth nodded; her smile almost playful. He chuckled, appreciating that she was trying to offer both of them a more comfortable situation.

"Who, if not I, deserved your disapprobation? That being said, you must know that your words bring me much joy. All I ask for is a chance to show you who I truly am. As to your proposal to talk or ask and not make suppositions, I not only agree completely, but I also welcome the chance as it allows me to talk more frequently with you, which is every husband's greatest wish, is it not?" For the first time Darcy's smile revealed his dimples and Elizabeth laughed, just as he had hoped.

'Oh my, this man is very handsome, especially when he smiles!' Elizabeth acknowledged to herself. "I am not sure that is the wish of every husband, and even should you come to regret it later, it is too late, you have already agreed." She teased him in return, winning his laugh in return. Yes, this was a much better start to their second day than either had suspected possible.

"When we were at Longbourn, I heard someone say that Mrs. Gardiner is renowned for her decorating skills. Would you like to wait to tour the house until she is with you?" Darcy asked.

"Yes, please, William; that would be perfect." Elizabeth was not oblivious. Not only was her husband pleased and much more relaxed by her decision, but so was she. It seemed that he would go out of his way to make her happy.

As they exited the dining parlour, they heard a knock on the door. When Payton opened it, Ladies Elaine, Catherine, and Jaqueline, along with Georgiana and Anne, entered.

"Ladies," Darcy bowed to his relations.

"We are not here to see you, William. Elizabeth, how soon are you able to get ready?" Lady Elaine asked.

"Where am I going, Aunt Elaine?" Elizabeth asked, preemptively smiling at the directness of her being the focus and that these ladies looked to be on a mission.

"You are going shopping with us. It will accomplish the practical purpose of your acquiring a new wardrobe while allowing you to be seen by London society with our approval," Lady Catherine commanded.

"It will not do for Mrs. Darcy to look like a country hoyden," Lady Jaqueline stated tersely.

"That is more than enough, *Lady* Smithson. You will *not* come into *our* house and insult my wife!" Darcy bit out, angry that the other arriving ladies looked scandalised by this woman's vitriol.

"Do you remember the penalty for bad behaviour towards your new cousin in public?" Lady Elaine asked her daughter-in-law acerbically.

"Yes, I do! We will lose our allowance for three months for each occurrence. In my defence, we are not in public here," the Viscountess could not help herself making a snide remark.

"How dare you call my wife a hoyden without having ever met her?" Darcy demanded. Elizabeth found that she quite enjoyed the umbrage her husband took with the woman who had insulted her. "And pray tell, *Lady* Smithson, what would you call one who violates his or her marriage vows, with more than one person? Any decent person believes one is too many," Darcy shot back at his cousin's wife, whose face turned red and pinched in such a way that he was reminded of the shrew, Caroline Bingley.

While Elizabeth ascended the stairs to change, Darcy asked his aunts to put as much as was needed for Elizabeth on the Darcy accounts. Suspecting that Elizabeth would be uncomfortable spending that much money, he further asked his aunts to make sure that she would have enough of everything. "Unlike some," he looked pointedly at the Viscountess, "my wife does not like to waste money just because of her station, and she especially does not make purchases she does not think she can cover. I believe it will be a great pleasure to spoil her as often as I can get away with just because she is so unassuming."

--*-*-*-*-*-*-*-*-*-*-*

"Cousin Mary," Collins pulled his cousin's attention from the book she was reading. "Do you object if I join you?"

"Please do, Cousin Collins, for I was not doing anything of consequence." Mary welcomed him with a smile, indicating he should sit as she blushed becomingly at having his full attention.

"What are you reading, if I may so bold as to ask?" Collins enquired.

"Shakespeare's *Much Ado About Nothing*," Mary showed him the cover.

"You seem to favour his comedies?" Collins noted.

"To tell you the truth, this is only the second of the Bard's works that I am reading. Papa recommended I start with the comedies after reading Fordyce, which he calls a tragedy," Mary explained.

"Fordyce was a fellow man of the cloth, but in my opinion, I would not recommend his work to any young lady. I like to write my own sermons and do not use other's words. Do not get me wrong, Cousin Mary, I occasionally look at others' sermons to get an idea, but then I write it in my own words trying to apply the lesson to my parishioner's lives. I own a copy of Fordyce's sermons, but it is a book that only gathers dust," Collins admitted.

"It seems that my copy will have the same fate now," Mary revealed. "Papa requested it from me, and I know not where he placed it. Will you not call me Mary without the cousin appellation before my name?" Mary blushed hotter at her forwardness but ached to hear him say her name, just her name. Making such a request was out of character for the middle Bennet daughter, but sometimes one cannot expect to understand ones hopes.

"I will be happy to address you as Mary as long as you call me William, or Collins if you are uncomfortable using my familiar name," Collins responded quietly. He assessed her as she looked away and found again that she was more beautiful to him today than she had been but the day before, which was a running theme during his stay. She was the most pious of the sisters and knew her scriptures almost as well as he himself, a clergyman, did. She was kind, and from what he could see, always striving to better herself.

She was not as pretty as her two older sisters. In fact until a few days into his stay he would have termed her plain, although that was not important as the attributes in her character that were all beyond reproach. Of late she was wearing less severe outfits, and rather than her hair being pulled into a tight bun she had started to style it. He had watched her most carefully, and he knew it was because of him that she had made such efforts, to gain his notice. As he looked at Mary, Collins realised that she was very pretty in her own right. It was as if he were watching his garden in spring as everything started to bloom. Mary Ben-

30

net was blossoming before his eyes and everyone else's.

"I accept, William," Mary said softly, his name almost a caress that made his heart pound with the hope to hear her say it again.

"Please continue with your reading, Mary, though I may sit with you a while as you do, if you have no objection." He murmured and she smiled at him, returning to her book. As she was reading, Collins remembered the conversation that he had with his cousin the day that Mr. Jones had called.

Mr. Hill had requested that Collins join the master in the study and Bennet had indicated that he be seated.

"Before you came, I thought that I would be vastly amused by you as my only reference was your late father," Bennet had told him. "Instead, I have found an intelligent man who is a pleasure to have as a guest."

"Your words warm my heart, Cousin. My father's description of you and the Bennet side of the family could not be more at odds with the reality that I have found at Longbourn. The best thing that ever happened to me was going to live with my aunt and uncle. You may have noticed that I do not partake even in a glass of wine." He had noted and Bennet had nodded. "After my father and his penchant for the bottle, I have never touched any," Collins had informed his cousin.

"The reason that I requested you to attend me this morning is that there is news I must share in fairness to you. Depending on the result, it may affect you greatly." Bennet had offered a careful smile.

"Are you talking about your wife being with child?" Collins asked insightfully. At Bennet's eyebrow arched in question, he had added, "I have seen enough parishioners in that state to be able to recognise the symptoms."

"If we have a son, you will no longer be the heir-presumptive," Bennet had stated with a note of apology in his voice.

"It will be by His will. If He gives you a son, I will be first to wish

you and your son well. Unlike my late father, I have never coveted Longbourn. I love my work as a parson and will not be sorry if I remain in that vocation for the rest of my days," Collins had said with complete sincerity.

"You are not the only observant one. Your attention to our Mary has not been missed," Bennet had stated. "My hope is that you are genuinely interested in her, and it has nothing to do with whether or not you inherit the estate."

"Bennet, I can assure you that my intentions are completely honourable and are in no way tied to my inheriting Longbourn. I do find that Cousin Mary and I seem to be very compatible, and I am developing tender feelings for her." He admitted.

"As long as it is her free choice with no pressure from any quarter, I will welcome you as a son, if you are the one she decides to spend her life with," Bennet had said earnestly.

"Believe me, Cousin, I am not one of those witless men who would try and press his suit after the lady has refused him. I get the feeling that Cousin Mary is not indifferent to me, so I requested more time away from Hunsford and it was granted as my curate is doing an estimable job in my absence," Collins assured his cousin.

"I do have one request, Collins. In the case that our new babe is a girl, which given the five daughters previously the chances seem great, but in the event that we do not have a son, would you consider changing your name to Bennet? There have been Bennets on this land for many generations, and, if you agree, I would like to see Longbourn remain in the hands of a Bennet," Bennet had asked.

"As I am not particularly attached to my father's name, that would be easy for me to grant, if it comes to that eventuality. You have my word of honour on that, Cousin." Collins had stood and extended his hand which was gratefully accepted by Bennet.

Collins smiled as he watched Mary Bennet and enjoyed the different emotions playing over her face as she was reading. 'I will not rush you, Mary,' he promised himself. 'It is imperative that you knows your own mind, and that you will understand what will *be expected of the wife of a clergyman.'*

*_*_*_*_*_*_*_*_*_*_*

Five of the six ladies who set out to shop returned to Darcy House more than six hours later. None of the others had uttered a word of opposition when Lady Smithson had requested to be returned to Matlock House halfway through the shopping expedition, claiming an indisposition. There was no doubt that the sullen woman was prevaricating; she did, however, do the remainder of the shoppers a favour as their enjoyment was far greater with the Viscountess' absence.

Anne de Bourgh had sat most of the time while they were out however, and still she was fatigued by the time they arrived at Darcy House, so Elizabeth asked Mrs. Payton to show her cousin to an entrance level bedchamber. Georgiana had told her of their existence, so Miss de Bourgh was able to get some much needed rest within moments of it being possible.

During the time at the various modistes, mantua makers, and sundry other stores, Elizabeth and Georgiana had become close enough that they were addressing one another informally. Georgiana had felt comfortable enough to share with Elizabeth that she did not like the family nickname of Georgie, so Elizabeth suggested Giana, which Miss Darcy loved and told her new sister that she would request that everyone use the new nickname rather than the one she detested.

Due to her separation from the family, Lady Catherine did not know her young niece very well and Georgiana had always been intimidated by her aunt. Lady Elaine informed her sister that Elizabeth was doing wonders drawing out their niece, who sometimes suffered from debilitating shyness. The Countess could not remember a time that she had seen Georgiana happier.

For her part, Elizabeth had been horrified at the amount of money that was being spent on her. Her husband had had the right of it, she had tried to order the minimum number of things, but Ladies Elaine and Catherine, with input from Georgiana, made sure that sufficient numbers of items were ordered at each shop. If Elizabeth had been aware of the actual amount of money that had been spent on her during that single day, she would have suffered an apoplexy.

Elizabeth rang for tea, and her husband entered the drawing room at the same time that the service did. Elizabeth was surprised to discover that she was pleased to see him. "How was your first foray into shopping with your aunts and sisters?" Darcy enquired after he received his cup of tea. It was then Darcy's turn to be pleasantly surprised. Elizabeth must have been paying attention at Netherfield Park because she prepared his tea exactly right, without having to ask him his preference.

"It was a most enjoyable time, especially after one of our party became *indisposed* and chose to return to Matlock House," Lady Elaine responded before Elizabeth could.

"It was enjoyable, except for the measuring, poking, and prodding," Elizabeth told her husband, smiling at him so he knew that she had not suffered too much. "I was not comfortable, spending so much money on myself."

"Quite peculiar for a young lady not to love shopping," Lady Catherine opined.

"I do have a suggestion," Elizabeth stated. "Before we go shopping again, let us visit my Uncle Gardiner's warehouses. He supplies many modistes and mantua makers with fabric. We would be able to get first pick of new bolts that have not been seen by any other."

"Oh yes," Georgiana clapped her hands, "that sounds like a wonderful plan, Lizzy. Please may we go, brother?"

"There is no reason why not, Georgie," Darcy agreed.

"William and aunts, I do not really like my name shortened to Georgie, it is a man's name, and one in particular I despise. I prefer Giana," Georgiana asked nervously, and Darcy did not miss how his timid sister looked to his wife for moral support.

His wife would be as good for his sister as he would be for himself.

"If that is your preference, *Giana*, then I have no objection. You may have to bear with me as I get used to the change," Darcy smiled at his delighted sister, who had been concerned that he may think her too impertinent.

"May we join you when you go to your uncle's warehouses?" Lady Elaine asked.

"You are most welcome, Aunt. I was not sure if you wanted to meet my family in trade at the warehouses near Cheapside," Elizabeth worried.

"You forget that we met your uncle and aunt at the wedding, and they are estimable people with whom we would like to become better acquainted," Lady Catherine replied. That was the last response that Darcy had expected from Lady Catherine.

"Why do you not send a note to invite them to call on you here as we discussed earlier, Elizabeth. I hope dinner on the morrow would not be too short a notice; then we may plan for a time to see the wares," Darcy suggested.

"If they accept for tomorrow and we are welcome, we would love to join," Lady Elaine informed the Darcys.

"We can celebrate Richard's resignation from the army," Lady Catherine remembered.

By the time the Matlock House party departed an hour and a half later, tentative plans had been made. Anne herself was much revived when her cousins wished her farewell after her rest. Elizabeth sent a note to Gracechurch Street, asking the groom to wait for a reply. He returned with a happy acceptance of dinner from the Gardiners and was then sent to convey the news to the Countess of Matlock.

CHAPTER 4

"Thomas, how do you think our daughter is faring in her marriage?" Fanny Bennet asked with concern one afternoon about a fortnight after the wedding.

"I was concerned for Lizzy, but I think they will end up doing well together," Bennet opined.

"How can you say that? I used to think that finding a wealthy man was the only thing that counted, but I was wrong. Our Lizzy needs to respect her partner and she could barely tolerate our son-in-law on their wedding day," Fanny Bennet worried.

"You will see, Fanny. Our second daughter will end up having all that she ever desired, and I do not mean materially. The day after the kiss he stole at Lucas Lodge I could see how much he longed for her to accept him. Did you not see how besotted William was with our Lizzy by the time they were married? He would walk though fire to make her happy. If our daughter can move past her prejudices and see the real man behind the mask, the one I glimpsed, then I am confident that she will not only respect him, but over time she will grow to love him," Bennet postulated.

"Mama, Papa? I have a letter from Lizzy," Jane told her parents as she entered the drawing room, her smile one of the biggest they had seen since Lizzy's marriage. Mr. Bennet's 'I told you so' look made his wife roll her eyes before she refocused on Jane. "Here Papa, you may read it to Mama."

7 November 1811

Darcy House, Grosvenor Square
London

My dearest sister,

I can already hear you as you read this, Jane, saying that you told me that you knew how it would be. And it is as you portended, for I believe that I am coming to like my husband. No, I do not love him, but, Jane, there is truly nothing that he will not do for me!

Before the wedding, I dismissed his talk of falling in love with me as stuff and nonsense, but it is true, Jane! No man would be as solicitous of his wife if he did not love her most ardently.

On the carriage ride to London, I was still looking for the worst motives in anything he said or did, but I had an epiphany during that first night at Darcy House. I hold the keys to my happiness in my own hands, and that as long as I look to find fault in him, I will find it whether it is there or not.

"What did I tell you, Fanny? As soon as she was willing to set her prejudices against our son-in-law aside that she would start to be happy," Bennet chuckled when she waved aside his words and nodded at Jane to continue. For Bennet's part, even more than being proven right, he felt a great deal better knowing that his daughter was not miserable.

Did you know that William has arranged for us to spend Christmastide at Longbourn? I was so embarrassed; I initially berated him for not asking my opinion first, and he gently responded that he had wanted to surprise me. That helped me see that I was part of the problem. I compared him to his late nemesis! I thought I had asked a legitimate question, but I did not need to bring that hated man's name into it and did so only out of spite.

When I saw his anger, and more than that the hurt I had caused him, it was enough to make me re-evaluate my attitude. Do you know what made me feel even lower? He did not remonstrate with me; he instead thoughtfully answered my question.

I woke up the next morning, and every morning since, deter-

mined to make the best of our life together. Not only is William far happier with my efforts, but so am I. We also agreed to no longer make assumptions; rather, we will speak to one another. He answers any question I pose fully, and never once has condescended to me. He truly does respect me, Jane!

On my first full day in residence I went shopping, and no, Mama, I did not get styles that could be enhanced with much lace. For my choices, I had the benefit of counsel from the Countess, her snarky daughter-in-law (picture Miss Bingley with a title—she, too, is one none in her family have time for), Lady Catherine, Anne de Bourgh, and our new sister, Giana. (She asked to be called that name rather than Georgie.)

What I actually ordered was, in my opinion, far too extravagant, but whatever I ordered it seemed my new aunts tripled or even quadrupled the quantity! Until I saw Darcy House and the fact that the cost of things does not bother my husband at all, I do not think that I had much idea of how wealthy he actually is. Remember, I refused his invitation to sit with him and Papa when the marriage settlement was signed. I have since seen a copy. Do you know that he settled <u>fifty thousand pounds</u> on me? I cannot even imagine how much that is, nor would I be able to spend such a sum in five lifetimes! And, to my relief, he has said that our daughters will have dowries in the same amount that Georgiana has.

"Thomas, you did not tell me that William settled such a sum on Lizzy," Fanny Bennet fanned herself. "How large is Miss Darcy's dowry?"

"I believe that Georgie—no Giana, has thirty thousand pounds, Mama," Jane replied.

"He has more than ten thousand does he not, Thomas?" Fanny Bennet asked in shock. She had a hard time conceiving of anyone with so much wealth.

"A lot more than that, Fanny. Let me continue reading." He looked back at the letter in his hand.

We had a dinner at Darcy House, to which Aunt and Uncle

Gardiner were invited. The Fitzwilliams (the Earl, Countess, and **Mr.** Fitzwilliam) and the two de Bourgh ladies also attended. Yes, I did not err, for Richard is no longer in the army. In preparation for his marriage to Anne and becoming the Master of Rosings, he resigned and sold his commission of his own accord and with the expectation of enjoying every second he was able to with our cousin Anne.

We have had meals at Gracechurch Street twice, and all of the Gardiners (yes, our nieces and nephews are part of that all) have spent the day here with us, and we had a family dinner at Matlock House a few days ago that the Gardiners were invited to.

A week after the wedding, Giana and Mrs. Annesley moved back into Darcy House. She is such a sweet girl. I believe that she would enjoy Mary and Kitty's company unless Mary has a reason not to leave Longbourn at this time. Jane has told me about the attention that our Cousin Collins is paying to my sister, which may mean that she prefers to stay there.

I want to specifically note that no one has looked down at Aunt Maddie or Uncle Edward because of their ties to trade. They are treated as they now are, honoured members of the Family! Aunt returned the day after the first dinner with the girls and was with me when the housekeeper (Mrs. Payton) gave us a full tour. You know what a good eye Aunt Maddie has for décor, so I particularly wanted her guidance.

You will see, soon I hope, that although everything is the best quality, it is a home. My husband gave me carte blanche to make any changes that I see fit, and many would have spent unnecessarily to display things no one wants to see in a vain assumption that wasting money on ugly objects projects wealth, as Miss Bingley would have done. Aunt Maddie agrees that, besides my chambers, there is little to change.

I believe that the housekeeper was afraid that I would turn the house into some monstrosity as others might, for she breathed a sigh of relief when outside my chambers I only ordered a little updating of four guest chambers which had the wallpaper peeling a little.

My husband overheard two maids commenting on my being out of my depth given my 'country upbringing and clothes.' He wanted to dismiss them on the spot, but I restrained him. We instead assembled all of the staff and William told them, in no uncertain terms, that he would not tolerate any gossip about me or any other member of the family. He also informed them that any more rudeness to me, who has his full and unreserved support, would lead to summary dismissal without a character. He offered anyone who felt they could not work under the rules a character if they chose to leave that day. No one did. The two maids are now my biggest supporters after William told them that were it not for me, they would have been let go.

Hello, Papa, for I am sure that Jane is allowing you to read this missive. I decided to leave the best for last. I know that you prefer not to leave Longbourn, but I am about to provide an incentive for you to do so. Darcy House has a library that houses ten to twenty times as many books as you have crammed into your book room. That on its own would be enough, and in this one instance Miss Bingley did not lie.

The library at Pemberley holds hundreds of times MORE tomes, Papa! As much as I love you, I will not place a bed in any of our libraries for you. Papa, you cannot imagine the number of first editions that William has!

Jane, please, you must let me know how your courtship with Mr. Bingley is proceeding, and I cannot wait to see you. William joins me in inviting all of you to Darcy House if you feel up to a trip before Christmastide.

Your loving sister,

Elizabeth Darcy

"In my opinion, we must make the journey to assure ourselves that our second daughter is truly well," Bennet stated, the mischievous glint in his eye making his wife smile at his daughter.

"And I assume Lizzy's description of the library at Darcy

House has nothing to do with your sudden urge to travel to London, a city you dislike intensely," Mrs. Bennet smiled. She had to admit that it would be good to see her second daughter and assure herself that Elizabeth was doing as well as the letter intimated.

It had never sat well with Bennet that there had been no choice but to force Elizabeth to accept her marriage to Fitzwilliam Darcy. They would have weathered the scandal had he not believed it the right thing to do, so reading the genuine feeling with which his favourite daughter wrote lightened his burden over her forced wedding. He would not feel completely absolved, however, until he could see that she loved her husband in return. A marriage of unequal affections is a burden he did not wish on anyone. Yes, he wanted to see the library, but his main concern was his daughter.

"Should I write to let Lizzy know that we are accepting her invitation?" Jane asked.

"No, Jane. You know how I like to surprise people," Bennet replied.

"Thomas!" his wife admonished him. "Should we not allow Jane to write?"

"I am sure that Lizzy expects this. I will wager that everything will be ready for us as she knows her father far too well," Bennet grinned. And so it was that the order to pack was issued, and the carriage was made ready for travel the next day.

Later that day, Bennet's prediction was proved correct when a large and extremely plush Darcy traveling coach pulled up at Longbourn. The driver stated that his mistress had ordered him to stay until the family wanted to journey to London. "Yes," Bennet lamented at Elizabeth's thwarting his intent to surprise her, "Elizabeth definitely knows me far too well!"

--*-*-*-*-*-*-*-*-*-*-*

If it were not for the fact that she would have to clean

up after herself, Caroline Bingley would have ripped the offending London gossip pages to shreds and broken any glassware in sight. "That should have been *my* life!" she complained aloud to no one.

There had been a steady diet of articles that mentioned the new Mrs. Darcy and how she had been seen all over town with the Countess of Matlock, Viscountess Smithson, Lady Catherine, Miss de Bourgh, and Miss Darcy. How could that country nobody be accepted so readily by people she had long wanted to meet but to whom she had never gained an introduction?

The tirades over what her niece read had reached an alarming level, so Aunt Hildebrand told her butler that after the papers were read by herself, they were to be burnt. The range of colours that Caroline's complexion turned when she read the news caused her aunt to be concerned that the younger lady would give herself an apoplexy.

Despite this step, and though Caroline never saw another London broadsheet or gossip rag lying around, she had seen enough to renew her resolve to find a way to get her revenge on a country nobody who had taken the life that she had dreamed of for so long.

Unlike her brother's study, her aunt's office was always kept locked. She never considered that her brother would have warned Aunt Hildebrand of Caroline's penchant to steal, and the frustration of not being able to rifle through the office for funds with which to make her escape was yet another thing she blamed Eliza Bennet for. Despite knowing who the hated woman had married, there was nothing that would induce Miss Bingley to use the hoyden's married name, as it would not stay that way!

--*-*-*-*-*-*-*-*-*-*-*

Bingley, having a standing invitation to Darcy House, joined the Bennets for their first journey to Grosvenor Square. "Good Lord!" Mrs. Bennet exclaimed when she first caught sight of her daughter's house in Town. "I thought Lizzy's letters had prepared me, but if anything she understated the magnificence of this house!"

Her husband had shared the truth of their son-in-law's wealth with her, but until the instant Fanny saw the house, it had been abstract to her. She found it difficult to grasp just how wealthy a man with more than twice his reported income was. Fanny started to get an idea as she looked around the square. There was only one other house among those surrounding his which seemed to rival Darcy House in size.

Jane cringed at her mother's exclamations, but she had to own that in the not far distant past her mother's effusions would have been vulgar about the cost of all that she beheld. Jane was relieved to see that was no longer the case; her mother seemed intimidated.

As soon as the most comfortable coach that any of the Bennets had ever ridden in came to halt at the base of the steps, it was attended by several footmen. Bennet exited first and then handed his wife and three younger daughters out. Bingley was next out and he claimed the honour of handing his angel out. The front door was held open by Mr. Payton. When the Bennets entered the hall, they found the master and mistress of the home waiting for them.

"Welcome to Darcy House," Darcy intoned as he shook his father-in-law's hand. "I trust that your travel was comfortable, Mrs. Bennet." The matron was beyond surprised when the man that she remembered being taciturn and aloof kissed her cheek!

As Elizabeth hugged her father, she was pleased to see how welcoming her husband was to her family. "As soon as I mentioned the library in the missive, I asked William if I could send one of our carriages," Elizabeth told her father happily.

When Fanny Bennet assessed her daughter's day dress, which was of the finest quality and proved that the lace she always preferred was unnecessary, and as she looked around Darcy House, she finally understood what her daughter meant by 'understated elegance.' As she waited her turn to hug Elizabeth, Fanny relaxed. It was obvious to see that her daughter was happy.

"I was complaining to one and all that you know me too well, Lizzy. You spoiled my surprise," Bennet mock scolded his second daughter.

When Fanny hugged her second daughter, she held the embrace for a long time. "How well you look, Lizzy. I am so happy to see that I need not be more than a little concerned about you, as mothers never stop worrying for their children."

"Thank you, Mama, I too missed you. It is pleasurable to see all of you," Elizabeth answered, not yet relinquishing her mother who she had started to like just when she had been required to leave.

"Is it acceptable that I made use of your open invitation to me, Darcy?" Bingley asked.

"My wife anticipated that you would be with the party from Hertfordshire, so your usual chambers are ready for you, my friend," Darcy grinned at his best friend.

"Who are you and what have you done with Darcy?" Bingley ribbed him. He could not remember Darcy ever being this ebullient.

"Mary, where is Mr. Collins?" Elizabeth asked as she hugged her middle sister.

"He has returned to Hunsford to assist his curate in preparations for Christmastide." Mary blushed becomingly when she mentioned the man that she was beginning to have tender feelings for. "He will return the day after Christmas."

Elizabeth hardly recognised her two youngest sisters. They were neither boisterous nor vulgar in an attempt to gain attention. They had waited patiently and demurely until it was their turn to greet their sister, new brother, and his younger sister. '*I will have to ask Jane what has changed at Longbourn, for it is obvi-*

ous that it is not only my life that has been transformed.' Elizabeth told herself.

"Mrs. Payton will show you to your chambers. You are, of course, being housed in the family wing. When you have washed and changed, just ask any of the footmen or your maids to direct you to the yellow drawing room," Elizabeth told her family.

"We have our own maids?" Kitty gasped, for a moment forgetting her manners. "Sorry, Lizzy, I was caught unaware."

"No harm done, Kitty," Elizabeth smiled at knowing the spirits were still there but were being appropriately tempered. Once her family had gone to refresh themselves in their chambers and Georgiana made her way to the music room, she turned to her husband. "Thank you for the warm welcome of my family and assisting me to make them feel at home, William."

"They are my family too, Elizabeth, and it is their due to be treated with the same respect as members of my side of the family are," Darcy smiled down at his wife.

"You will not have to wait much longer, William," Elizabeth promised softly as she slid her hand into his and gently squeezed to reassure them both.

"When you are ready, you will let me know, Elizabeth." He leaned toward his wife, and she lifted her head toward him not averse to experiencing the first kiss that she desired. The butler cleared his throat before their lips met reminding them that they were not alone. The footmen on duty in the hallway looked everywhere but at their master and mistress.

CHAPTER 5

Elizabeth appreciated the effort that her husband was making to be friendly throughout the invasion of the Bennet Family. He had been welcoming and solicitous of their family's needs. During the first full day of the visit, Elizabeth gave those who wanted one a tour of Darcy House.

The first stop on the tour was the library. "I think I will forgo the rest, Lizzy," Bennet said as he marvelled at the floor to ceiling shelves filled with his friends of old. Yes, he had started to exert himself rather than disappear into his study for all hours of the day at Longbourn, but he was a bibliophile and could not pass up the opportunity to thoroughly investigate the room he now found himself in. "You say the library at Pemberley makes this one look small?" He asked with such reverence his family all smiled at his obvious pleasure.

"That is what I have been told, Papa," Elizabeth responded.

"You have not been misinformed," Georgiana offered shyly. "The collection has been added to over the generations. The library at the estate is many times larger than this one."

Bennet soaked in the sight of the neatly packed shelves, estimating the size of the room to be near that of a small ballroom. "When will you be at Pemberley, Lizzy?" Bennet asked, unable to look away from the sight before him.

"I am not sure, Papa, but I will let you know when I speak to William," Elizabeth smiled. She had known that she would lose her father to the library, and was pleased he was so happy, not noticing that her husband had entered the library behind them.

"While the ladies see the rest of the house, I would be happy to explain the layout to you, Bennet," Darcy offered. His offer was accepted with thanks.

"You do know that I will not accept you sleeping in the library do you not, Thomas?" Fanny Bennet teased.

"Yes, dear, I am aware of that," Bennet feigned despondency making her laugh in return.

Elizabeth had heard that the relationship between her parents had continued to improve, but she was nevertheless surprised at the level of connubial bliss that her parents seemed to share. She left the men in her life to their books and led the ladies, and Mr. Bingley, out of the library.

The first stop was the floor that housed the family apartments. Elizabeth, with Georgiana's help, showed her mother and sisters the family floor that included a sitting room which was considerably larger than the largest drawing room Longbourn could boast of.

"Giana, I have heard that this house is nothing in size to Pemberley's manor house. How can that be? This house is enormous!" Mrs. Bennet asked as they neared the end of the tour. The final stop was the ballroom, which was two to three times the size of the one at Netherfield Park.

"It is quite a bit larger than Darcy House," Georgiana answered softly.

As she listened to the conversation, an idea was forming in Elizabeth's mind. *I want to talk to William, but what if we have Christmas at Pemberley? It is still more than a month away, so there should be no issues with having the house ready for guests!* Elizabeth resolved to talk to her husband as soon as she could.

When the tour ended, Elizabeth found her husband who was still with her father in the library and requested a moment of his time. For a moment he was worried something had gone wrong, but her smile alleviated his fears.

"Would my study suit?" Darcy asked and his wife nodded. "This way, Elizabeth." Darcy interrupted her departure as he pushed the corner of one shelving unit and there was a click. The unit swung open to reveal a portal to the master's study. "My grandfather, like my father and myself, loved books so he had this built to easily access the library from the study," Darcy explained to his wife and father-in-law.

"Does that mean that anyone who knows how to open it may disturb you in your study or vice versa?" Bennet asked, enjoying the house with so many interesting possibilities more than he had believed he might.

"If I am desirous of privacy, there is a locking mechanism in the study that prevents the shelf from swinging open," Darcy explained to both his wife and her father. The Darcys stepped into the study where he pulled a lever that swung the shelf back into place. When Elizabeth inspected the panelling in the study, she saw that if she had not known it was there, she would not have believed it, for there was nothing that gave its existence away. "You asked to talk to me, Elizabeth?"

"Yes William, I had an idea. I find that I would like to see my new home in Derbyshire sooner rather than later. As things stand now, we would return to Town after Twelfth Night and stay here for the season, or at least part of it. Is that not correct?" Elizabeth asked.

"That is the current plan," William smiled, guessing her hope.

"With Christmastide more than a month off, is it too late to celebrate the holiday at Pemberley?" Elizabeth searched his expression so she would not miss any hint of displeasure, even were he not to speak of it.

"There is more than enough time to organise what needs to be done. I thought you were pleased at the idea of being with your family for the holidays?" He asked in confusion.

"I said nothing about not being with them!" Elizabeth

arched an eyebrow as the realisation of what his wife was suggesting sunk in.

"What about the members of the family who normally celebrate at Longbourn with your parents? And did I not hear that Collins is returning soon to spend Christmastide with the Bennets?" He detailed his few concerns so they could come to a conclusion that worked for them both.

"Is Pemberley's house not a large one?" she teased him.

"Do you truly want to have everyone with us? Since my mother and then my father passed, Christmas has been a lonely affair at Pemberley, but I believe that it is time to change that. We can also invite the Fitzwilliams and the de Bourghs to make it a full family holiday," William enthused.

"What of Richard and Anne's plans to wed in December?" Elizabeth asked, wanting to ensure nothing would affect their plans.

"I can safely say that I believe neither of our cousins would object to marrying a little bit earlier. I know that Aunt Elaine would be happy with Richard resigning from the army earlier than he had planned. Before you believe me to be pushing, remember I owe them both for being in the way, even unintentionally. This would be my restitution. Although I would not be able to give back all the time they have had to wait, it will be a blessing and a relief to be able to *suggest* that they do."

"Which also means that the Smithtowns would be with us." Elizabeth could not imagine how the snobbish viscountess she had met and the imperious husband she had heard about would treat her relations in trade.

"That is not an issue, Mrs. Darcy, for as luck would have it those two spend the season at her father's estate, far, far away from Pemberley," Darcy grinned.

"In that case, let us plan," Elizabeth nodded, her eyes bright with excitement. Her husband closed the distance between them, and her breath caught as he tentatively reached out to take her hands, watching her intently to make sure that she was not uncomfortable.

Elizabeth heart was racing. William intended to kiss her, and she found that she welcomed the thought. William almost pushed her against the panelling as he leaned past her to lock the secret portal. After locking the door, he lifted her effortlessly to sit on his desk and cupped her face with his hands sending a frisson of excitement through her body.

"May I..." Darcy murmured. Before he could complete the question, Elizabeth leaned forward and brushed his lips with her own. She blushed the deepest colour that Darcy had ever seen at her initiating the contact. His arms snaked around her waist as hers found their way around his neck.

He lowered his lips; the kiss was chaste but was more than a mere brushing of lips. When he pulled back to gauge her response, her soft whimper of displeasure made his heart pound in his chest. Her fine, captivating eyes stayed closed, and she leaned into him searching for his lips with her own. Unable to resist her request, he captured her lips again, and his tongue swept across them as he tasted her.

When she opened to offer entry, she gasped at his tongue's tentative touch against hers. He retreated, gasping when her tongue followed his and slid along the tip. He pulled her tighter into him as he gently suckled on her tongue in a bid to keep it, groaning when she pulled away.

"Had I known how much I would enjoy kissing you, I would not have waited so long," Elizabeth offered softly as she stared up at her husband. "Come to me tonight, William, please."

Darcy thought that he had died and gone to heaven, he was so happy. There was no doubt that his wife was no longer indifferent to him and they were going to consummate their marriage! He kissed his wife on her forehead, knowing that if he tasted her sweet lips again, he would take her up over the stairs immediately, company be damned. "Tonight but do ask that your bath be prepared before we go up, Elizabeth. Please." He swallowed dryly when she laughed.

"I think I should return to the drawing room. My family will think that I am lost in our house as I have been absent for so long." She teased him into a grin.

"I need a bit of time before I am fit for any company other than yours." He watched her, relieved she did not shrink from his wanting her.

With a tinkling laugh, Elizabeth exited her husband's study via the door that opened to the entrance hall.

--*-*-*-*-*-*-*-*-*-*-*-*

Bennet was not overjoyed that he had been summoned from the library, but he joined the family and Bingley in the green drawing room with no more than a scowl at those who had summoned him. Elizabeth served tea then put her proposition to the family.

Bennet's first inclination was to refuse so that the Darcys would be able to celebrate quietly as he had wanted to with his Fanny their first Christmas at Longbourn, then he remembered the treasure waiting for him at the other end, so he decided to wait for his wife's preferences before he made his own known.

"I have always wanted to see Pemberley in the winter," Bingley shared. "However, I intend to spend Christmastide wherever Miss Bennet will be."

"My sister and brother and their families are to be invited, Lizzy?" Mrs. Bennet asked.

"Yes Mama, as is Cousin Collins." Elizabeth smiled at Mary as she said the last and Mary's responding smile lit up the drawing room.

"If Hattie and Edward agree to come, then we will also. So far to travel in the *small* Bennet carriage," Mrs. Bennet hinted, somewhat subtly when compared to how she had been only weeks before.

"As we have a few, I will send the same coach home with you and then it will be available to transport all of you to Pemberley," William offered, and his mother-in-law was indeed pleased. To be seen riding around Meryton in the Darcy carriage would be the least he could do for her since he had indeed compromised their daughter, which may have been the best thing he had ever done. To allow her the pleasure of being seen so treated, it was the least he could do for the woman who had birthed and raised his Lizzy. "You will be able to use your carriage for the trunks, should you desire, Bennet."

"William," Georgiana called out, surprising her brother with her boldness although it obviously pleased him greatly. "Did you not tell me that mother used to hold a ball for Twelfth Night?"

"Yes, Giana, it is true that she did. As I was telling Elizabeth, it is time that Pemberley came back to life. Twelfth Night falls on the Sabbath, so we can hold a ball on the Saturday, the fourth day of January," William suggested.

"Darcy, are you well?" Bingley asked with a grin. "You do know that you are suggesting to *host* a ball where people dance and that you would have to be sociable to those you invite to your estate, do you not?" Bingley's question was pointed and only partly in jest.

"We do need to drop Lydia off at her school in Wiltshire by the tenth day of January. I suppose if we depart Pemberley the Monday after the ball, the four plus days will give us enough time to arrive at the school on time," Bennet mused.

"From the estate, unless we are snowed in, four days is more than enough time," Darcy informed Bennet.

"Aunt Maddie and Uncle Edward will be joining us for dinner today, so I can ask them their thoughts," Elizabeth acknowledged her mother's desire to have her brother and sister with her as had occurred almost the whole of her life at Longbourn.

"I will write a letter to Aunt and Uncle Phillips, and we will see the de Bourghs and Fitzwilliams when we go shopping on the morrow. I will deliver their invitations in person," Elizabeth enthused.

"Please let me know when your letter is ready, Elizabeth; I will have a groom ride to Meryton and he will return with the Philips' answer," Darcy offered.

"Thank you, William. I will go and write my note so he may arrive before nightfall," Elizabeth stood and left the drawing room.

While Jane had hoped that Lizzy was happier with her situation, as the last letter she received from her younger sister seemed to indicate, what she observed pass between her sister and new brother seemed to be more than had been intimated. There was a warmth there that she had never observed before. Jane excused herself and followed her sister out of the drawing room to the mistress' study and closed the door.

"Lizzy, for the first time since before the compromise you look genuinely happy. I have seen you make as if you are happy before, and this is not that," Jane observed.

"It is happiness, mayhap more than. Oh, Jane, not an hour ago we shared our first kiss—and I more than liked it, I wanted more of him!" Elizabeth blushed profusely.

"Did I not always tell you that he was not the man you made him out to be, Lizzy?" Jane smiled knowingly.

"You were right, Jane. I am starting to develop tender feelings for William. When we got married, I believed that the best I would be able to do would be to tolerate him. But even more, I invited him to my chambers tonight!" Elizabeth's excitement was tinged with nervousness, but Jane ignored the latter to help her sister focus on the former.

"Your first kiss and your first night together all in the same day? Not many women can boast such, my dear sister. I believe I would be let down if you had followed convention at this point." Jane teased her sister into a laugh. "Why did you wait so long, Lizzy? You liked him when you wrote, and I know that your courage always rises when something is as intimidating as that would be."

"William has not claimed his marital rights; he left it up to me. He is truly a good man, Jane. Never once did he try and pressure me to do anything that I have not wanted to. You know we always wanted to love our husbands, and I wanted to know that I at least could love him a little. When our mother would be desperate for our father to notice her and he was desperate to be away from her, we saw what an unequal marriage was like. That they have found happiness again is a relief, but for myself I wanted not to hurt him by being distanced in such a moment as he clearly loves me. I wanted to be able to let him see that I liked or even loved him when I asked him to come to my bed."

"That was truly kind, Lizzy, but I will not be able to look at either of you when we break our fasts in the morning knowing that you will become a wife in every way tonight!" She squeezed her sister's hand in appreciation of her foresightedness. If she were to give her all to a man who could not look at her, her heart would break, and she knew Mr. Darcy's would had Lizzy forced herself.

"I felt like a wanton when he kissed me, and I find I care not. All I want, even right now, is to get closer to William. While I will never like the way we were forced to marry--you know how I hate to be forced to do anything contrary to my inclination-- I am reconciled and I wonder if it will, in the end, be for the best." Elizabeth forced herself to focus on the here and now rather than the night ahead as it served only to make her regret the hours left before bed or wish there were twice as many.

Elizabeth wrote her missive and the sisters returned to the drawing room where she handed William the note. Their hands touched. They looked at one another in surprise to see if the other, too. had felt the jolt of electricity. Neither withdrew.

"Would you two like the rest of us to leave," Bennet quipped, intentionally breaking the moment for everyone's sake, most specifically his Lizzy's who blushed. William rang for Mr. Payton and instructed him to dispatch a groom with the note. He was to return with a response.

*_*_*_*_*_*_*_*_*_*_*_*_*_*

After the Gardiners arrived at Darcy House and had been seated in the drawing room for a while, Madeline Gardiner noticed there was marked difference in Elizabeth's relating to her husband. There was no missing the looks that passed between Elizabeth and her husband. Wariness had been replaced by looks of tenderness, and Mrs. Gardiner was happy for her niece. Evidently Elizabeth had taken the advice she given her niece to heart, that she controlled her own happiness.

While everyone was sitting in the yellow drawing room waiting for the butler to announce dinner, Elizabeth issued the invitation to Pemberley for Christmastide. "I would love to visit Pemberley again," Mrs. Gardiner admitted happily, "it will, however, depend on Edward and how long he is able to be away from the business."

"It will not be an issue, Maddie. I have no pressing matters expected until after the new year," Edward Gardiner confirmed.

"Now we just need to wait for Aunt Hattie's response," Elizabeth offered to the group at large.

"Mrs. Gardiner, did you say *visit Pemberley again*?" William asked.

"First, as you are married to my niece, please call me Aunt or Maddie. I am not *that* much older than you, Mr. Darcy. Second, yes it would be again for I grew up in Lambton. My father was the late reverend, John Worthington. My father would meet with your late father, and on occasion I accompanied him," Mrs. Gardiner explained.

"Of course, you were Miss Maddie Worthington. Until she became sick, mother would at times assist you with your piano-forte lessons," Darcy's eyes lit up.

"You knew my mother, Mrs...Aunt Madeline?" Georgiana, who particularly loved to hear about her mother, asked hopefully.

"I knew your late mother quite well. You look so much like her, Giana," Mrs. Gardiner told the younger girl. "When we have some time alone, it will be my pleasure to recount my memories of your mother for you."

"I would love that. Thank you, Aunt," Georgiana's excitement was palpable.

Aside from finally be able to show his wife that he loved her, this day was proving even more special because Darcy witnessed the way that the Bennets and Gardiners were drawing his sister out. He had never seen her willing to speak up in company before, and it gave him infinitely pleasure to know that she was overcoming her fears and shyness with such encouraging family as was theirs.

Dinner was a lively affair, something unheard of at the pre-wedding Darcy House. Just as Elizabeth rose to lead the ladies to a drawing room, Upton proffered her the silver salver. "Aunt and Uncle Philips would like to come, but their carriage needs replacement."

"They may use my carriage, may they not, brother?" Georgiana immediately volunteered the option.

"Thank you for the quick solution, Giana. Her coach is a similar to the one which conveyed you to London, only smaller," Darcy informed the Bennets.

"In that case, I will inform them of the offer in the morning," Elizabeth stated.

In the drawing room there was much excitement and planning for what they might do for the upcoming travels, and in the dining room with his cigars and brandy, Bennet was daydreaming about the library. He was so lost in thought that Bingley had to shake his shoulder to get his attention when the men stood to re-join the ladies.

As soon as it was acceptable to do so, Mr. and Mrs. Darcy pleaded fatigue and departed for their chambers. Bingley and Jane caught one another's eyes and despite the fact that they wished it were them, they could not be happier for their two favourite people finding the love that neither had expected to discover.

CHAPTER 6

Upton was waiting when Elizabeth entered her chambers. Quickly divested of her clothes, Elizabeth climbed into the bath; when she stepped out ten minutes later, Upton had laid out the flannel night gown that she wore every night. "Not that one tonight, Upton. Please fetch the yellow silk one that my Aunt Gardiner gifted me. I will also want the robe that goes with it," Elizabeth instructed.

If Upton was surprised by the change that her mistress ordered, she did not show it. She helped Elizabeth change and then brushed out her mistress' hair, as she had each evening since her mistress' arrival. "Should I plait your hair, Mrs. Darcy?" Upton asked.

"No, Upton, I think I will leave it down. You are excused for the night. I will ring for you when I require your assistance in the morning," Elizabeth replied.

Elizabeth then looked in the mirror to make sure that what her husband would see was the image she hoped she presented, and in doing so glimpsed her maid's small smile as she left. Yes, the house would know; it was impossible to avoid that, but tonight was for them as husband and wife, and she wanted her husband to show her that he wanted her now that she had grown to want him.

There was a knock on the door that led to the sitting room. "Enter," Elizabeth called, the butterflies in her stomach fluttering faster. The sight of her barefoot husband, dressed only in a white lawn shirt open halfway down his chest and breeches took her breath away. Elizabeth owned that her husband was the most handsome man she had ever seen.

She marvelled at the sight of his uncovered neck, but even more so at what she could see exposed of his well-toned chest. His upper chest was covered in short black hair, which she suspected continued downward, though she could not yet say for sure.

Elizabeth did not miss the bulge in the area of the falls of the breeches, then admired how muscular his legs were. When she met his eyes after her perusal of him, she saw his hunger, and her own deepened.

Before Darcy knocked, he had been in the sitting room counting the seconds until the hour was up. His whole body felt alive with anticipation. He was driven to knock on the door five minutes early because he could not stand the uncertainty of her changing her mind. To his relief, he was bade enter.

As if she had read his thoughts, she stood there with her chestnut tresses unrestrained, cascading freely on her shoulders and down her back. She wore the sheerest of cloth, the outline of her womanly assets making his mouth go dry and salivate at the same time.

As his gaze drifted lower, he saw the dark triangle that disappeared between her legs and could barely force his eyes back up to hers, but needed to again confirm his welcome, her own hunger making his deepen with the desire to satisfy her every need.

"William, I want to see all of you," Elizabeth demanded as she licked her lips in anticipation. William undid the buttons of his white lawn shirt; his eyes locked with his wife's as it slid off his shoulders and pooled on the floor. His hands moved towards his breeches, but they stopped before reaching their goal. "Remove your robe, please, Elizabeth," he requested, his voice husky with desire.

Elizabeth allowed her robe to fall to the floor without hesitation, as she marvelled at the view of her husband's bare chest.

She had presumed he was muscular, but nothing prepared her for the sculptured man that stood before her. She had heard that William thought nothing of doing physical work when needed, and his arms, chest and stomach bore witness that it was fact.

As she followed the tapering chest hair that now disappeared into his breeches, Darcy soaked in the vision that was his wife without her robe. Her nightgown was so sheer that it left nothing to the imagination. He licked his lips when his eyes rested on her breasts, discovering that she was either aroused or cold, or both, as her pert nipples looked hardened which caused his member to start pulsing, demanding to be free of its constraints; he knew that if he did not settle this would be over far too soon for either of them.

"Your breeches, William!" Elizabeth demanded. Darcy obeyed her order then stepped toward his wife, whose eyes were wide and riveted on his erection. He was relieved that that he saw no fear, and pleased he found she was almost breathless as desire started to override any best intentions. William had always suspected that Elizabeth had depths of passion, even if she was unaware of it; he was seeing proof that his hypothesis was correct. He was awed and felt privileged to be the one she would explore that passion with.

When he was close enough and saw the welcome in her eyes, he slid the sheer nightgown off her shoulders, appreciating the unhindered view. He rested a hand on her side and with a light touch, requested she come to him, needing to have her close the remaining distance of her own volition. When she did, he marvelled at the feel of her nipples against his chest.

Elizabeth was lost in a haze of need, and the sensation of her breasts skimming over his chest caused her to gasp. Then, she felt the heat of his erection against her stomach and instinctively pressed against it, wining his sharp intake of breath as her prize.

She raised her face to beg him for she knew not what

and his lips captured hers, the kiss an expression of their separate hungers they needed the other to fulfil. Weeks of pent-up emotions and passions were poured from one to the other as it deepened in strength, their arms wrapping around one another in a need to keep close. Their bodies were consequently pressed together, and when she shifted slightly, he groaned and tried to still her even as a drop of white, milky liquid spread along the head of his member and onto her skin.

"I need you, Lizzy." He ground out, his breath ragged with lust and longing.

"Make me your wife, William," Elizabeth begged.

"I will have you in my bed, Elizabeth. I need to have you there." William lifted her carried her past the sitting room and to the enormous bed in his room placing her in the middle, relieved that she had opened herself to welcome him as he positioned himself above her. "I love you Lizzy," Darcy murmured, capturing his wife's lips before she could respond, as he could not hear that she did not love him just then. He then pulled back to lock their eyes as he obeyed his wife's command as often as she asked.

--*-*-*-*-*-*-*-*-*-*-*

When Elizabeth awoke wrapped in the arms of her softly snoring husband who was lying behind her. They were both naked, and Elizabeth found that she was comforted at being in such a state with her husband even in the light of the day. She was a little stiff and sore, but nothing more.

As she considered the whole of the night, she remembered her husband's declaration of love. It pleased her to know that he loved her, but they both knew she was not in love with him—yet; she appreciated that he had not asked her to lie. However, after their first night of relations which had made them irrevocably husband and wife, Elizabeth believed that falling in love with William was not just a possibility, rather a probability!

She would not lie to her husband by verbalising feelings she did not possess, but when she had the chance, she would tell her husband that she had feelings of a tender nature for him, and that was but a short step away from love if it is given the chance to become such.

These last weeks had proven she would have a felicitous marriage, something that until a few short weeks ago she had ben certain was an absolute impossibility. When she considered their combined future now, she only could envision respect, happiness, and love. She was quickly coming to realise that not only was William a good man, but, in fact, one of the best of men.

As gently as she was able to, Elizabeth extricated herself from her sleeping husband's warm embrace then stood and looked back at him. How handsome he was! She refreshed herself and found that the morning cold was more than enough motivation to hurry back to the warmth of the bed.

Darcy opened one eye as felt his wife exit the bed, watching her naked form retreat into the bathing room. Seeing her walk away from him confirmed that last night had not been but a dream; the signs of his wife's lost maidenhood on the sheet was additional confirmation of all they had shared. He had admitted to Elizabeth that he loved her, and while he could not have borne hearing she did not return the emotion, he was relieved that she didn't look away from him as he had made her his wife. He was sure that her feelings for him were growing, but he would not push her in that. He hoped to hear her say those same words to him one day, but he wanted to hear them *only* when it was a truth freely given. He was certain his wife's character would only permit her to make such a declaration if she felt it strongly —not merely a vague inclination.

By the time Elizabeth was crossing the room, Darcy was propped up on one elbow admiring her form as she returned to their bed. Rather than hurry back like an embarrassed maiden, when Elizabeth saw he was watching her, she slowed and exaggerated her walk so he could look his fill. She saw his eyes darken in hunger. She watched him in return, needing his passion. They both were pleased to see that even here in the light of day, the fires of passion burnt brightly in them both.

--*-*-*-*-*-*-*-*-*-*-*-*-*

The master and mistress rang for their personal servants just before ten, at least three hours later than their wont, and Darcy also had a footman bring them a tray to break their fasts. Neither Chandler nor Upton were surprised to be summoned so late, given the behaviour of the two the previous night. Chandler noticed the traces of blood on the sheet in his master's chambers, so he removed it before the maid that cleaned the master suite could see it. He, like Upton for the mistress, was very protective of his master's privacy.

After the quick meal, Upton helped her mistress to wash and dress for the day. Elizabeth wore one of her new winter day dresses and was very much looking forward to the day with their family.

When the smiling couple entered the yellow drawing room, Ladies Elaine and Catherine were waiting, looking at them expectantly. Elizabeth suddenly remembered the shopping trip which had been scheduled for an hour earlier. As Elizabeth scanned their amused expressions, she held each gaze in confirmation of what she could not openly admit.

"I will join my father-in-law in the library," Darcy stated, beating a hasty retreat after he had greeted everyone present.

"My apologies for forgetting about our shopping trip," Elizabeth said. She would not apologize for what had occurred, no matter who had been waiting.

"While we waited, we have been furthering our acquaintance with your mother and sisters," Lady Elaine smiled at Elizabeth. "Are you ready to depart, or should be reschedule?"

"There is no reason to reschedule, Aunt Elaine," Elizabeth said, smiling pleasantly. "But as I am the cause of the delay,

I shall be buying the tea today," she challenged, smiling when Lady Catherine's laugh filled the drawing room as she looked at Elizabeth with pride and appreciation.

"I say we make that a standing custom--the cause of the delay buys tea. Thankfully, I myself am always punctual." She offered with the haughtiness of the woman she had been before Darcy had compromised this young woman so they would get to claim her as part of their family. She was startled to hear genuine laughter from her daughter.

"It has been too long, Cat, and it is nice to see you again. May I introduce you to your daughter, Anne. Anne, I would like to introduce you to my sister-in-law and your mother, Cat." Elaine laughed at Catherine's affected effrontery then she rolled her eyes.

"I suppose that was fair, for I did lose my sense of humour somewhere. Send out the Bow Street Runners and promise them a hundred pounds if they return it to me intact," Catherine declared, winking at Fanny, and causing her to lose her fight for composure, the shock of it making Elaine laugh with her.

"You are the cause of everyone's happiness, Lizzy. They have not laughed like this in a long time, and it is only possible because you are happy." Jane walked to Elizabeth and took her hand. "This is your gift, Lizzy; you bring happiness to all those who know you."

"I was sure there was some mention of a shopping trip, so if you ladies are done..." Elizabeth drawled, smiling when even Jane could not help but laugh as she walked with her Lizzy, the two of them leading the others toward the entrance hall.

Not too long after, the ladies all set out for Bond Street. Darcy would have preferred to spend the day locked away with his wife, but he was enjoying getting to know his father-in-law. Bennet informed Darcy that Bingley, who he knew was not one to sit in a library, was in the billiards room with Mr. Fitzwilliam.

An hour later the men departed for White's where they

planned to have their midday meal with the Earl of Matlock, who was waiting for them. They had also decided that would meet the ladies later in the afternoon at *Giuseppe's* for hot drinks and pastries.

*_*_*_*_*_*_*_*_*_*_*_*_*_*_*

Caroline Bingley had been frustrated at every turn as she attempted to find a way into her aunt's study. Not only was the door always locked, but an intimidating footman was always on duty close by. The only explanation was her weak-spined brother must have shared her penchant to *borrow* funds with Aunt Hildebrand.

There was only one avenue left for Caroline Bingley to gain funds: the few pieces of her mother's jewellery that were in her possession. Caroline was loath to sell the pieces that were a connection to her mother, but her desire to exact revenge overruled any second thoughts she may have had. She did not know how she would do so yet, but she would have to get her aunt to agree to allow her to go into the city. Once there, she would arrange to visit one of the jeweller's stores. She would have to convince her escort, because Aunt Hildebrand would never allow her to sally forth on her own. As soon as she could, she would sell some of her precious jewels.

Once she had the necessary funds for a one-way trip, she would need to find a way to slip away without being apprehended by one of her aunt's brutish footmen. But she would plan that afterwards.

Before she took care of Eliza Bennet, Caroline would demand from the family solicitor that he release her dowry to her so she would be able to leave England after her revenge was complete.

CHAPTER 7

After a sennight in Town, the Bennets returned to Longbourn, any worry about Elizabeth's felicity having been assuaged. There was no denying that the Darcys were happy together.

Kitty and Mary had become remarkably close to Miss Darcy. Mary and Georgiana had music in common, while Kitty shared the interests of both sketching and painting with her. Slowly but surely during the days the Bennets had been at Darcy House, Georgiana became more comfortable in a larger group. At the dinner for the Bennets the previous night, Georgiana had performed for an audience that included the Bennets, Darcys, Fitzwilliams, de Bourghs, and Gardiners. In the past, she would never have agreed to perform for more than one or two at a time, and only for those who were closest to her.

To no one's surprise, when the three young ladies had taken leave of one another, there had been many hugs, and a few tears. The three friends were consoled by the fact that they would all be together at Pemberley within a fortnight and had promised to write one another and exchange letters.

Lydia, for the most part, had kept to herself. Since she had realized how close she had come to ruining herself and her family, the youngest Bennet had been subdued. She had accepted going to school without any argument because she felt that it would give her a chance to discover who she truly was. She prayed that who she discovered would be someone she could be proud of, as she could not be during the last three years.

Upon returning to Netherfield, Bingley first greeted his

elder sister and her husband, informing them where they would be spending the Christmas season. After he had changed, he retired to his study, thinking about the object of his affection, Jane Bennet. Since his request for a courtship with his Jane was granted, there was hardly a day that he had not been in her company.

During their week in London, they had grown closer than he thought a week would allow. He had observed how concerned his angel had been over her sister's happiness after being forced to marry Darcy. He had the privilege of watching her worry dissipate as his promise of Darcy caring for Mrs. Darcy was proven true. It was obvious to all that their marriage would see both of the Darcys happy.

He had taken pleasure in giving Miss Bennet and her mother a tour of the Bingley townhouse on Curzon Street. The home was far smaller than Darcy House and not in such a fashionable area, but that had not been of concern to his angel. She had been diplomatic about Caroline's gaudy and ostentatious style of decoration and had blushed most becomingly when Bingley had told her that his wife would be free to redecorate and turn his house into a home once again.

The more time that they were together, the more certain Bingley was that he was irrevocably in love with Jane Bennet. He had a strong suspicion that she was in love with him too, even though they had never canvassed the subject during their many conversations. Whenever they were in each other's company, they gravitated toward each other as if there was an unseen force that drew them together.

'So, what am I waiting for?' Bingley asked himself. 'Jane is not mercenary, of that, I am sure. If she does not love me, she will not accept me. Is that why I am waiting? Am I afraid that she would reject my proposal? That is an unreasonable fear!' he berated himself, not knowing yet that any man in love would fear the same thing. It is those who do not love their prospective bride that do not fear the possibility of a rejection, possibly even hope for one! Bingley sat up straighter in his chair and resolved to not allow cowardice stand in the way of his future happiness. He thought about asking Darcy and his sister's opinion, and just as quickly dismissed the thought. *'I do not need anyone's opinion; this is something that only Jane and I can decide! So there is only one thing I can do, I must propose to the woman that I love and pray she will accept me!'*

Bingley found the Hursts in the drawing room and was glad to be able to share his news with someone now that he had made his decision. "I am going to propose to Jane Bennet and make her my wife, if she will have me." He stated firmly.

"The only surprising thing is that you have waited this long, Charles," Louisa smiled at him, her amusement telling him everyone likely expected this news, and he was the one dragging his feet.

"Well then, go to it, brother," Hurst urged, "for you will accomplish nothing toward your aim standing here."

"Then I have your approval?" Bingley asked as he looked from one to the other.

"Do you need it?" his sister asked.

"No, no, I do not, but I would like to have it nonetheless as she will be part of our household," he explained.

"Of course you have it, Charles; I think that Jane is ideal for you," Louisa said as she stood and hugged her brother. "Go to her, Charles, and bring her home to us as soon as may be. I have long been jealous of the kinship the Bennet sisters share, and I would be grateful to have one for my own!"

Bingley practically sprinted into the hall while calling for his horse, pointedly ignoring the sounds of laughter in the drawing room he had vacated. He needed little assistance in gaining his saddle, so excited was he, then took off for Longbourn. Now that he had made his decision, he could not wait to put the question to his beloved Jane.

When he was shown into the drawing room, he greeted the Bennets, smiling warmly at Miss Bennet, who returned his with such a smile that stole his breath. Once he had forced himself to look away, he saw that Mr. Bennet was not in the drawing room, so Bingley excused himself and made his way to the master's study.

Hearing a knock, Bennet called out "enter," arching an eyebrow in question when Bingley entered with a steely look of resolve one can only have when firm in one's position and set on a decided path. Bennet had no delusions; this was the day his Jane would put another man before him in her heart. "What can I do for you, Bingley?" Bennet enquired with a steady gaze of his own.

"Mr. Bennet, as you know I have been courting Miss Bennet for above six weeks," Bingley began.

"I am acquainted with that fact. "Is it your purpose today to relay facts to me that I already know?" Bennet smirked at his soon to be second son-in-law,

"No sir," Bingley agreed. "I am here to request a private interview with Miss Bennet."

"What is your intention if I grant you an interview with my oldest daughter?" Bennet asked, knowing full well what the younger man wanted to ask his daughter, but he was in the mood to have some sport with Bingley.

"To ask for her hand in marriage," Bingley stood tall. "Miss Bennet is the only woman who I have ever truly loved, and I will strive to make her happy for the rest of my life."

"You are in a position to afford a wife, are you?" Bennet asked the expected question for that was one thing he must be certain of, though in truth he already was.

"Very much so, Mr. Bennet. You have heard that my income is between four and five thousand pounds, have you not?" Bennet allowed that it was so. "It is actually between six and seven thousand per annum. My father left me a legacy of close to one hundred and fifty thousand pounds. I will use that to purchase an estate with a profit above six thousand pounds. I intend to settle thirty thousand on Miss Bennet so she will have pin money of above one thousand pounds per annum." Bingley was relieved when he saw Bennet's surprise. It was obvious Bennet had not expected such determination from the young man.

'He is no puppy,' Bennet thought, 'Yes, he will do very well for our Jane.' "You may have your private interview with my daughter. Wait here while I summon her," Bennet stated as he rose and walked toward the door. "Do not touch my book, as I do not want to lose my place," Bennet ribbed the man he was sure would be his son-in-law soon enough.

To Bingley it seemed like an eternity while he waited, but in truth it was not above five minutes. His face lit up when Miss Bennet was shown in, accompanied by her father. "You have ten minutes, and the door *will not* be fully closed," Bennet stated and left his study, allowing the door to close but two thirds of the way as he left.

"You requested my presence, Mr. Bingley," Jane stated, her heightened blush telling him that she was both affected and expectant of this being as significant as the request implied.

"I did." Bingley dropped to one knee and took her hands in his own. "Miss Bennet, Jane, I am in love with you, and find that I do not require any more time to know my mind. At first it was your countenance that captured my attention, but the more I have gotten to know you, the more that I could see that your physical beauty is nothing to your beauty within. You are compassionate, generous, and care so much for the welfare of others. You are an angel in truth, and I hope to be able to call you my angel.

"I know that you were worried about your sister Elizabeth, and I did not miss how much you were able to relax once you saw for yourself that the words in her letter were in fact borne out by deeds. The fact that your sister's and others' felicity is so important to you is but one of the myriad things I love about you." Bingley paused and did not miss the look of unadulterated pleasure that Jane Bennet showed.

"If you need more time I will wait, and for as long as you need. If you do not want me to continue courting you, I need to know that too. It would break my heart, but if I am not the one who can make you happy, I will withdraw. If, as I hope, you too love me and do not need more time, please relieve my suffering, as it is my heart's desire to be your husband," Bingley implored.

"Yes, Charles, I do love you, and yes, I want to be your wife more than anything in the world. I require no more time, and in truth have been hoping that you would propose for some weeks now," Jane responded. The perfect joy she showed when gazing at him filled his very soul.

"Tell me you will not want a long betrothal, my angel," Bingley begged as he again stood. When she took a breath to reply he captured her lips with his own. Jane's arms wound around her betrothed's neck, and she pressed into him, unwilling to let him go.

The two of them were so lost in the spell of this first chance to express their love that they failed to hear the knock on the door. Bingley started to pull away from Jane, but she instead kept him close and met her father's eyes, silently telling him that she was unashamed of her actions. "What I just witnessed had better mean there is a betrothal. Does your action mean that a special license is to be presented after a short betrothal?" Bennet asked with an arched eyebrow.

"There is no need, Papa. I very happily accepted Mr. Bingley's proposal," Jane informed her father, daring him to censure her for kissing the man she loved.

"In that case, you have my consent and blessing," Bennet smiled ruefully at the beaming couple. "Do not let me *catch* you taking liberties with my daughter in that fashion. Welcome to the family, son."

"He took nothing that I did not willingly give, Papa," Jane told her father firmly.

"At this point I am not sure who coerced who! I would suggest that your betrothal period not be too long," Bennet said with resignation.

"Mama will not be happy if it is under three months," Jane opined.

"What say you if we get married in January?" Bingley asked?

"We will only depart Derbyshire after Twelfth Night, unless…" Jane looked at Bingley.

"We marry at Pemberley?" Bingley asked and Jane nodded. "Do you not want to marry from Longbourn?"

"That would mean marrying at least a month later." Jane shook her head. Bennet sat silently and watched as his most serene, and he had thought biddable, daughter exerted her opinion. "You do not wish to wait another month do you, Charles?" Jane challenged. "All of our family will be present. The only others I would wish be there who are not already invited would be the Lucas family, and I have the feeling that Lizzy would not need any convincing to invite them to Pemberley."

"The Darcys depart London in two days. We need to send them an express before they begin their travels. Mr. Bennet, may I use your desk?" Bingley asked.

"Oh no, Charles; I will write it. I have heard all about your handwriting, and I want William and Lizzy to be able to read the letter," Jane teased him.

"So it begins, son," Bennet chuckled as Bingley raised his hands in supplication. Jane sat down at his desk and wrote the missive, and Hill was charged with sending a groom to Darcy House.

"With that done and allowing no one to change our preference, I believe it is time to acquaint my mother and the rest of the family with our news." Jane again stepped to Bingley's side.

Mrs. Bennet and her younger daughters looked up when Bennet, Jane, and Bingley entered the drawing room. There was no mistaking the way that Jane and Bingley were holding hands nor the glow of happiness that seemed to emanate from them. Bennet still made the announcement, despite the fact that the occupants of the drawing room expected it.

"Oh my Jane, I knew that you could not have been so beautiful for nothing," Fanny Bennet said as she hugged her daughter. Much to Jane's delight, there were no additional vulgar effusions or blatant allusions to her betrothed's wealth. "Have you decided when you want to marry?" Fanny asked after the congratulations had been made.

The proposed plan was shared, and rather than wailing and moaning about not having enough time, or a demand from Mrs. Bennet that they go with her about the neighbourhood to show off her good fortune, there was a calm response. "If that is what you choose, Jane, you have my full support. It is your wedding, after all."

Bennet was pleased at his wife's calm and rational response. "Do not forget, Fanny, that we still need to hear from the Darcys," he pointed out, tempering the expectations of all in the room until they were certain they could gain their wishes.

--*-*-*-*-*-*-*-*-*-*-*

"An express from Longbourn," Elizabeth worried as she hurriedly broke the seal. As she read, her husband saw her face transform from concern to pleasure, and he could barely mask his surprise when, without a word, Elizabeth handed her husband the missive.

Darcy read:

19 November 1811

Longbourn

Sister and Brother,

Congratulations are in order. Charles proposed and I have accepted him! We are in love, which I know you are aware of, and I could not be happier. My betrothed wanted to write the express, but I decided that it would be better if I performed the office, as this is too important a request to allow any confusion.

"Wise woman, your sister," Darcy quipped. "We would never have been able to decipher the scratches, blots, and smudges Bingley calls handwriting." He read on.

We do not want to wait too long to marry, and so have a request of you. Would you agree to allow us to marry from Pemberley before or after Twelfth Night? All of the family will already be present. I would hate to marry without Charlotte present, so that would necessitate inviting Sir William and family to Pemberley, should you agree to our request.

The groom will wait for your answer.

Lizzy and William, I thank you in advance,

Jane.

"Unless you object, Elizabeth, I see no reason not to answer in the affirmative," Darcy smiled after reading the brief letter.

"Object! No, William. I am extremely grateful that you agree," Elizabeth gushed.

"There are close to sixty bedchambers at Pemberley, so please tell our sister that she is free to invite anyone from Meryton that she desires to be at her wedding," Darcy added.

"I will, William, though I do not believe she will want to invite anyone other than Charlotte's family. They are the family that we are most intimate with in the neighbourhood." Elizabeth rose and kissed her husband on the cheek before walking to her study to write her response.

She was no longer surprised that her husband would be so accommodating. Since being at Darcy House, her estimation of William had increased by leaps and bounds. And to her own relief, after the night of their first coupling, their personal relationship had grown strong.

From that night, Elizabeth used her chambers for everything but sleeping. Nights were spent in her husband's bed, and she found that she enjoyed sleeping in his arms each night, and the intimacies they had discovered were beyond anything she had imagined possible.

While Elizabeth believed she was not yet in love with her husband, she owned to herself that she was close. When she said the words she was well aware her husband was hoping to hear, she wanted to be able to promise him that they were true.

Other than his wife telling him that she loved him, Darcy was the happiest that he had been. He had always suspected that Elizabeth was passionate, but the reality far outstripped the dream. Soon they would be on their way to Pemberley, and he could not wait to show their estate to his wife that he adored.

CHAPTER 8

William Collins arrived back at Longbourn just after midday a few days after Jane's betrothal. After washing and changing out of his travel attire, he joined the family in the drawing room. In addition to the Bennets, Bingley, the Hursts, and Miss Lucas were also present. It did not take long before he learned that his cousin Jane had accepted Mr. Bingley's proposal. Collins congratulated the happy couple as he settled on a sofa near Miss Mary.

"Now that I have read some of Mr. Shakespeare's tragedies in addition to a few comedies, I can tell you that I do prefer the comedies," Mary opened the conversation with Collins in continuation of a previous discussion during his first visit at Longbourn.

"Have you read any of the Bard's sonnets yet, Mary?" Collins asked.

"Not as yet, William," Mary admitted. "However, I have been told my brother Darcy has a magnificent library, and we depart for Derbyshire in a few days."

"I thought that the family would celebrate Christmas here?" he asked, concerned his time with Mary would be cut short.

Bennet, who was sitting nearby, heard the conversation and realised that he had been remiss in writing to his cousin with the change in plans to tell him the Darcys extended an invitation to Pemberley. "Collins, I must plead old age. I meant to forward you the invitation from my daughter and son-in-law but forgot. Christmas had moved to Derbyshire, and all who would have been here are invited."

"And there will be a wedding," Kitty added, smiling at Jane and Bingley as it was obvious to all that they were in love.

"I also understand that most of the Fitzwilliams, as well as Lady Catherine and Anne de Bourgh, though I believe she will be Anne Fitzwilliam by then, will be attending as well." Bennet added.

"She is now," Collins informed them. "I married them in a small ceremony yesterday. Lady Catherine and the Earl and Countess of Matlock were present. For some reason, the Viscount and Viscountess did not attend."

"You have not had the pleasure of meeting the Smithtowns yet, I take it, cousin?" Bennet asked. Collins shook his head to indicate that he had not. "If you met them, you would understand that you missed nothing. The wedding means that Mr. Fitzwilliam is your patron now, I believe."

"Yes, he is. The Lady Catherine I initially knew would not have been so sanguine about relinquishing her role as mistress. She has been very gracious, so much so that Mr. and Mrs. Fitzwilliam would not hear of her being relegated to the dower house and insisted that she remain in the manor house with them," Collins related.

"When do you have to return to Hunsford, William?" Mary asked.

"By the middle of January, cousin, so it seems that I am able to attend the celebrations in the north." Collins was gratified to see her pleasure at his confirming that he would join them. "Is there enough room for me, or will I need to travel post?" Collins asked.

"There will be more than enough room!" Bingley, who was sitting close to Collins, exclaimed. He then explained that besides his carriage, the Bennet, Lucas, and two Darcy carriages would be used.

"My family is very excited to be invited for both Christmas and the wedding," Charlotte Lucas stated, as she had been conversing with Mary before Collins had sat down on the sofa with her. "We have never travelled north of Hertfordshire and London before. It will truly be a pleasure to see Eliza, as the last time I saw her was the day of her wedding."

As Lydia Bennet watched her family and friends enjoying one another's company another wave of guilt washed over her. Not for the first time she remonstrated with herself for what her selfish, immature behaviour would have cost her family, never mind herself! Rather than missing the praise that her mother used to shower on her as the favourite, she was happy it had ceased as she knew that it was both undeserved and the pronouncements her mother used to make were wrong.

Jane and Mary had taken her under their wings and were helping Lydia identify her past unacceptable behaviours. She also spent at least one hour a day with her father in his study reading and discussing the passage afterward. Her mother had told her many times that she was sorry for the incorrect guidance that she had given to Lydia and her other daughters. She sometimes allowed maudlin thoughts to overwhelm her, but Lydia was starting to believe that all was not lost for her.

--*-*-*-*-*-*-*-*-*-*-*

The Darcys and Mrs. Annesley had made good time on their trip since departing Town a little over two days previously. Thankfully, there had not been any significant snow yet, although no matter how well she was wrapped up in the vehicle, Elizabeth felt how much colder it was becoming the further north they travelled.

"This is Lambton." Georgiana pointed out as they entered a town. "It is but five miles from here to the estate."

"The town where Aunt Maddie grew up," Elizabeth added as she looked out of the windows on both sides of the carriage to see as much as she could. She was unsurprised to find that her aunt had described it perfectly.

"It is an amazing coincidence that her father, Mr. Worthington, was the parson here. The man who took over after his passing will be retiring soon, in a matter of months," Darcy informed the ladies.

"Did not Mr. Holden hold the living here, brother?" Georgiana asked.

"You remember details better than I, Giana, and I will be sad to see him retire. I will start the search after Twelfth Night," Darcy replied.

From what Elizabeth could see, Lambton was a market town not unlike Meryton. It was a little larger, but otherwise there was little difference. Exiting the town the carriages turned north-west and soon passed under an archway that proclaimed 'Pemberley' in large, brass letters.

The coaches travelled on Pemberley land for almost an hour and had not yet reached the manor house. Elizabeth was fascinated by the forests that she saw on both sides of the drive that seemed to go on as far as the eye could see. She could not wait to explore their paths during her future rambles. The drive made a turn to the right as they negotiated an incline. Just below the crest, Darcy rapped on the ceiling with his cane and there was a halt.

Elizabeth looked at her husband questioningly and then she noticed that both William and Giana were smiling. Darcy exited and handed his wife and sister down. Darcy offered each of the ladies an arm. Elizabeth wound her hand around an arm, as did his sister. They walked past the carriage and the team and arrived at the crest; It was then that Elizabeth was able to see the valley below.

On the west side of the valley, on rising ground, was the most enormous manor house that Elizabeth had ever beheld. From what she could see, the house was five stories with more windows that she had imagined a house could have. There was a garden behind the house that led to the foot of a tree-covered hill. The light of a weak November sun made the façade of the house glow with a golden hue.

Elizabeth could see where the drive turned into a roofed internal courtyard. She surmised the roof was a good idea, given the rain and snow in the north. In the front of the house were extensive gardens. Where the gardens ended, a grassy park began that extended down to a lake whose still water reflected the giant mansion.

As she looked around, she could see that the gardens were not contrived or overly sculptured. On the other side of the lake nature was unimpeded. Never had she seen a place that nature had done so much for. How little the awkward tastes of man had counteracted it!

"I am to be mistress of all this? I thought that Darcy House was large, but it a fraction of the size of this house," Elizabeth said, gazing at the manor in both awe trepidation.

"Remember it is but a house, Elizabeth. A large one, granted, but still a house. Just like Mrs. Payton was willing to help you assume your duties in Town, Mrs. Reynolds will be as accommodating, if not more so, here at Pemberley," William reassured her.

"What think you of Pemberley?" Georgiana asked.

"It is beautiful," Elizabeth replied with feeling.

"Then you approve?" William asked.

"Most certainly," Elizabeth responded.

"That pleases me greatly as your approval is not easily won," Darcy said with a smile that brought his dimples out.

"It is getting cold, William; may we continue on?" Georgiana asked.

"Of course, I should have considered that, but I was so excited for Elizabeth to get her first vista of her new house," Darcy explained with contrition.

"Do you ride, Lizzy?" Georgiana asked after they were seated inside the equipage.

"Not well, Giana," Elizabeth replied. "When I was eight, I fell off a horse and broke my arm. Since then I have relied on my feet to get where I needed to go."

"There are parts of Pemberley that are too far to walk; the park is ten miles around," Darcy informed his wife. "It would be my pleasure to teach you. I will find you an extremely docile mare."

"Mayhap it is time for me to try again," Elizabeth agreed. She decided that having her husband teach her would not be a bad thing and could not help but observe how much more William relaxed as soon as they were on Pemberley's lands. '*This is where I will see him at his best,*' she realized.

Elizabeth knew that she was falling in love with her husband. She was almost positive that it would be a matter of days before she was able to tell her husband that her feelings matched his own. When they had married, she had hoped that she might be able to tolerate being married to this man. Now she knew that they were perfectly matched.

The carriages passed under an archway into the internal courtyard. When they alighted, Elizabeth looked up at the roof that covered the courtyard and noticed that there was large panes of glass every so often above her head. They admitted natural light to the courtyard so that it was the same brightness as the outer courtyard.

When they alighted, the housekeeper, Mrs. Reynolds, and the butler, Mr. Finch, were waiting to greet them. Elizabeth thought that the housekeeper was possibly in her fifties and looked like a kindly lady. The butler looked younger. He had only been in his post some five years.

"Welcome home, Master William, Mrs. Darcy, Miss Georgiana," Mrs. Reynolds intoned. On entering the long hall that led to the grandest staircase Elizabeth had seen, she saw that the servants were lined up neatly in two rows to receive the master and mistress.

After the servants dispersed back to their duties, Mrs. Reynolds requested a quick word with her mistress, and they entered one of the morning parlours. "Are you happy with Upton or would you like to hire another maid, Mistress?" the housekeeper asked.

"Now that we are used to each other, I could not imagine a better lady's maid for myself. I choose her to be my permanent lady's maid," the mistress informed the housekeeper. Mrs. Reynolds thanked her mistress for giving her a few minutes before she had a chance to see her chambers.

Elizabeth noticed that there were two staircases. Her husband explained that one reached the family floor while the second one led to the guest floors. Similar to Darcy House there were three doors, but these were spaced further apart. Darcy led Elizabeth into the sitting room, which was more than twice as large as the one they shared in Town. The bay windows looked out over the hill behind the house. There was a balcony outside, but Elizabeth saw no access from the sitting room to it.

Darcy opened the door to his chambers, which were much larger than those in London. There was a twin of the bed he had in his chambers in Town. "That door leads out to the balcony. It extends to your chambers, where there is also a door to access it," Darcy explained.

Elizabeth looked at the bed with pleasure. As they stood in his bedchamber, Darcy tugged her to him, captured her lips with his and kissed her hungrily, for it had been three long days on the road. After the first few urgent kisses, they became slow and deep, soft. Elizabeth felt desire wash over her body in waves of pleasure, to every part of her tingling body. She responded with a natural sensuality which made Darcy thirst for more. It was this way each time that they allowed their passion its head.

If their sister were not waiting for them, they would have

shut the door to the rest of the world. As she was, restraint was necessary, so Darcy showed his wife her chamber, where Upton was unpacking her new wardrobe. The chambers at Pemberley were the same colour scheme as the ones in Town. Hers would be the first chamber she would redecorate at Pemberley. Before he returned to his own chamber, they agreed that they would meet downstairs in an hour, so that Darcy and his sister could conduct a tour of the house.

"Upton," Elizabeth turned so that she could access her buttons, "as long as you wish to remain in my service, I would like to offer you the permanent post as my lady's maid," Elizabeth informed her maid.

"Yes, thank you Mistress, I happily accept the position," Upton replied, her smile evident in her voice. With that settled, Elizabeth sank into a steaming bath. An hour later she was in one of her new day dresses with her hair up in a simple coiffure. Elizabeth had grown concerned that she would get lost when she went to find the parlour where they agreed to meet, but on exiting her room she made the fortuitous choice to exit via the sitting room. William was sitting in a wingback chair waiting for her.

"Thank you, William. I was about to look for a footman to direct me. Having you to guide me is much more pleasurable," Elizabeth told her husband.

"At your service, my liege," Darcy quipped.

"What did I do to deserve a husband who is so generous and solicitous? I am beginning to believe that we may have been fated to be together. Had it not been by compromise, it would have been through some other means." Elizabeth felt his tension ease as she rested her palm against his freshly-shaved face.

Darcy's heart was pounding so much so that he could hear it. It was the closest that Elizabeth had come to telling him that she loved him. He believed that they had been fated to be together, so hearing her say it but a month into their marriage excited him. But for the knowledge that Giana was waiting for them to join her in the music room, he would have picked his wife up and taken her to his bed. Had he known that his wife's thoughts were tending in the same direction, not even the knowledge that his sister was expecting them to join her would have restrained him. Instead, Darcy offered his wife his arm and they exited the sitting room.

"There you two are," Georgiana observed as the couple joined her and Mrs. Annesley in the music room. "Do you like my new Broadwood Grand, Lizzy? William gifted it to me for my last birthday, though I do not deserve such a gift!" she gushed.

"Yes, you most certainly do, Giana!" William enthused.

"Do not argue with William, Giana," Elizabeth teased, "for you know he is never wrong!"

"We should commence with showing our Lizzy her new home," William said chuckling at his wife's irreverent words.

The tour started on the ground level. Besides the music room there was the largest dining parlour Elizabeth had ever seen. She giggled to herself as she surmised that living at Pemberley, she would be seeing many 'largest she had ever seen' things. William explained to her that the parlour had been designed so that it could be divided into up to four sections of varying size. At its largest it could accommodate one hundred and forty diners.

There were four parlours and two drawing rooms in the public area that were used to entertain. They walked through the cavernous ballroom and followed Mrs. Reynolds as she showed the new mistress the kitchens and servants' areas.

Rather than the grand staircase, they took a second but no less ornate staircase that bypassed the family floor. It brought them directly to the second floor. The Darcy siblings explained that the second, third, and fourth floors had the same guest chamber layout. Also on each floor, along with twenty guest chambers, there were two sitting rooms.

The fifth floor was only accessible via the servants' stairs. The floor was divided into two sections, one side for each gender, and were serviced by separate stairs. After the guest floor, Elizabeth had requested to see the single servants' quarters; she was most impressed. It spoke well of the Darcys that each servant room had adequate space and was neat, tidy, and comfortable.

Darcy has left the best room for last--Pemberley's library. On the way down to the first floor, Elizabeth remembered that she had intended to ask her husband a particular question. "William, when my bath was being filled, I heard no servants emptying pails of water, and then as I exited the bath, Upton removed a stopper and the water seemed to run out. How is this possible?" Elizabeth asked.

"Have you heard of *indoor piping*?" Darcy asked.

"I did read about that somewhere," Elizabeth owned.

There is a boiler and a pumping system that supplies water to all bathing rooms on the family floor. Cold water comes from cisterns on the roof. This allows your maid to open two taps which can fill your bath anytime with no water being carted upstairs. One day the system will be extended to the guest bathing rooms, but that is for the future. For now, in the servants' hall on each guest floor, there are taps so that water is carried from there and not up the stairs," William explained.

"When did you add the system to Pemberley?" Elizabeth asked in wonder.

"My father initiated the project before his heart gave out and I completed it in his name." Both her husband and his sister looked sad at the remembrance of losing their father. They arrived at a set of double doors that Elizabeth judged were above the ballroom.

Darcy pushed the doors open and stepped back with a happy grin on his face for what he was about to reveal to his wife. As Elizabeth entered the library, her senses were assailed by the smell of leather from the thousands of tomes that she could see, and she was only seeing part of it. As they fully entered, it was clear that the lower floor of the library was above the ballroom and about the same size.

The library went two additional floors above the level that they were standing on. There were spiral stairways, one in each corner, that led to the floor above. The ground floor had bookcases arranged in the centre so that there was no wasted space. There were groupings of sofas, armchairs, wingback chairs, and tables placed near windows for those who chose to relax and read in the library.

The shelves on the walls on each of the three levels were floor to ceiling, so there were ladders on wheels for each section. "William this is truly beyond any description I had heard about this magnificent room! There are thousands upon thousands of books here," Elizabeth marvelled. "You do know that we will have to drag my father, Mary, and Cousin Collins out of this room for meals and to sleep, do you not?"

"I know your father is a fellow bibliophile, but I did not know about Mary and your Cousin," William replied as he took pleasure in watching her survey the room, her emotions spanning from awe and disbelief to amazement and wonder.

"It seems that it is not just piety that those two have in common; they both love the printed word. Mary has broadened her horizons since abandoning Fordyce's Sermons, thankfully!" Elizabeth clarified.

"I, for one, am happy that my new sisters will be arriving in a matter of days," Georgiana smiled.

"It is good that you are making so many friends, Giana," Darcy encouraged. "Elizabeth, when will you meet with Mrs. Reynolds about all the events we plan to hold at Pemberley over the next month?"

"We will start planning in the morning, William," Elizabeth assured her husband.

That evening, after a fine dinner and music from their young sister, Elizabeth and William retired to their chambers. After the second time that they had joined, as Elizabeth drifted off to sleep, she finally admitted to herself that she was in love with her husband.

CHAPTER 9

The next morning when Elizabeth awoke in her husband's arms as he softly snored, she realised that the feeling that she acknowledged the previous night was not due to the afterglow of making love. It was a new day, and Elizabeth was sure she had fallen in love with William, as sure as she had ever been about anything.

She was tempted to wake her husband to tell him again; she was bursting to say the words she knew he longed to hear above all others she could offer. Three simple words, yet the most powerful of words for those who knew what true love was. Regardless of the genesis of their union, Elizabeth had attained her dream, to be in love with the man that she married. To respect and be respected in turn.

Yes, the marriage had come before the love, but now she cared not. The only salient fact was that she loved William and he her. As gently as she could, Elizabeth slipped out of the welcoming circle of her husband's arms and made her way behind the screen to use the chamber pot.

She blushed a little as she walked back toward the bed to find her husband propped up on one arm, his dimples on display as he watched her naked form approaching the bed.

"Good morning, my love," Darcy watched his wife with mounting pleasure as his whole body enjoyed seeing her thusly.

"Good morning, my love," Elizabeth returned, as if she used that endearment as a matter of course.

"Did you sl…*WAIT*! Did you call me your love?" Darcy held his breath, hoping against hope that he had not misheard her.

Elizabeth slipped into the bed next to her husband, capturing his face in her hands. She drew his head to her so there faces were inches apart and William could see her eyes clearly. "I love you, William, I finally..." Whatever else Elizabeth intended to say was lost in an exuberant 'whoop' from her husband. Immediately after, he captured her lips with his own.

They loved one another multiple times, revelling in the physical manifestation of their love.

--*-*-*-*-*-*-*-*-*-*-*-*

"I missed you two at breakfast," Georgiana pointed out when her brother and new sister sauntered into the dining parlour for the midday meal. Georgiana smiled as her innocuous statement led to the couple blushing.

"We decided to have a sleep-in while we are able before our guests descend on us," Elizabeth covered, knowing that her husband hated to tell untruths. It was a small prevarication that would not harm anyone, and there was *some* truth to it.

The butler gave a light cough to announce his presence as he lowered a silver salver for the mistress. "It is from Jane!" Elizabeth exclaimed after thanking Finch and dismissing him. Elizabeth skimmed the missive, and seeing that there was nothing personal, read it to her husband and sister.

16 December 1811

Longbourn

Dearest Sister,

Charles and I want to reiterate our thanks for hosting our wedding at Pemberley.

By the time you receive this letter, we will be wending our way toward you. In addition to Charlotte's family, the Hursts, and of course our cousin Collins, our convoy will include Uncle and Aunt Philips, the Gouldings, and the Longs. We will meet Aunt and Uncle Gardiner and my nieces and nephews at the first inn we stop at on the Great North Road. Given the numbers that we travel with, and that some of them are young, we will not make haste. You should expect us around midday on Thursday, the ninth and tenth.

You must excuse mother. Once you and William stated that we could invite any from Meryton we desired, she took you quite literally. Papa was very gentle when he pointed out the expense of travel, so Mama did not sally forth with any more invitations.

I know that you told us of Pemberley's size, but I hope that we are not imposing on you, your husband, and sister.

It is so exciting, Lizzy. Mama is besides herself that I will be her second daughter married by special license. I cannot wait to see you, sister dearest!

With sisterly love,

Jane

"Elizabeth, I have just had an epiphany," Darcy exclaimed excitedly.

"What is it, William?" Elizabeth enquired as she arched her eyebrow at her husband's exhibition of youthful exuberance.

"When we were married in Hertfordshire, you were not pleased to be walking toward me and I was not happy about the pain I had caused you. What think you if we ask Bingley and Jane if they do not mind if we renew our vows and have a double ceremony? If you agree, this time we will both mean the words we speak, as the first time some of the words were spoken but not meant," Darcy suggested hopefully.

Elizabeth was reminded of her words to her husband when she told him that she had not been able to honour that one vow. "Yes, William, I think that is an excellent idea! There were so few present when we married, and both sides of the family will be here at the same time."

Georgiana was pleased as she correctly surmised that her brother and sister had fallen in love. By the time they departed Darcy House, Georgiana noticed that the palpable tension between them at their wedding was no longer present. It had started to reduce after their first week or two at Darcy House and had all but disappeared by the time the Bennets came to visit them in Town.

--*-*-*-*-*-*-*-*-*-*-*

Caroline Bingley had convinced her spinster aunt to allow her a day in Scarborough between Christmas and Twelfth Night. At last she could implement her plan! She would sell her mother's jewellery that day, then hire a carriage and a coachman. She did not want the coachman to take her money and not perform his task, having learned the possibility from the results of hiring that militia wastrel to compromise the conniving Eliza. This time she would give only a small part of the agreed upon payment, and the rest only when they arrived at their destination.

Miss Bingley was well aware that there was a high probability she would be apprehended, but she cared not. As long as she watched Eliza suffer, she would endure anything.

As she had no access to the post, Miss Bingley was not cognisant of the fact that Aunt Hildegard kept a close correspondence with her brother, and always knew where he would be in case she needed to contact him speedily.

Part of Miss Bingley's plan depended on stealth so she would not be caught before she reached the usurper. She intended to have the coachman collect her after midnight from her aunt's house. Hopefully, they would be halfway to her destination before the old woman realised that she was gone.

Given that the gaoler did not know she had anything of value, the house was not well guarded at night. The only night footman was the one keeping watch on her aunt's study. That would make it easy to slip away undetected at night.

For the first time since her exile, Miss Caroline Bingley felt some joy. In less than a month she would exact her revenge!

--*-*-*-*-*-*-*-*-*-*-*

Bennet thought himself prepared for the sight that greeted them as the Darcy carriage they crested the rise and gave its occupants their first view of Pemberley's manor house across the valley. He was wrong! There were gasps all around the interior of the comfortable vehicle when the view was revealed to them as they started their downward trajectory toward the house.

"My sister is mistress of all of this?" Kitty was the first to verbalise what they were all thinking.

"Rosings Park is nothing to this." Collins was awed by the beauty he saw before him. It was not the obvious wealth, but the natural beauty that drew his gaze. Where Lady Catherine's way had been to have every blade of grass manicured and, in its place, what he saw spoke of a harmonious balance between nature and man.

As each successive carriage in the convoy crested the hill, there were similar reactions. The only person in the group not overawed, aside from Bingley and the Hursts, was Madeline Gardiner, who had been to Pemberley a few times as a girl when she resided in Lambton. She had never been inside the house, but at least she was familiar with the vista. Their awe amused her, as she remembered well her own.

"My goodness, Thomas. I thought I grasped the depths of our son-in-law's wealth, but nothing prepared me for this!" Fanny Bennet shared as the carriage reached the bottom of the valley.

"If anything, our daughter's descriptions of her new home were understated," Bennet agreed. "It is actually possible that the size of the library may not have been an exaggeration!"

As the lead carriage pulled into the internal courtyard, the occupants saw Elizabeth, her husband, and Georgiana waiting for them on the top of the stairs that led to the big double doors. Elizabeth hardly had a chance to hug her parents and sisters before she was mobbed by all of the arriving guests.

"Welcome to Pemberley," Darcy managed to say above the

din of guests talking over one another to discuss what they saw.

"Our housekeeper," Elizabeth indicated the grey-haired woman behind her, "will show you all to your chambers. Charles, Mr. and Mrs. Hurst, you are in the same suites that had on your previous visit to Pemberley."

"Will you please call me Louisa?" Mrs. Hurst requested. "In not too many days we will be family, after all."

"I will if you call me Elizabeth or Lizzy," Elizabeth returned warmly.

"Eliza Darcy! You did not tell me that you live in a castle," Charlotte Lucas teased. "I will be lost for days in this mansion before any know that I am missing!"

"You will find your way around just as I did. It is a big house, but as Giana pointed out, merely a house. How are you, Charlotte? I am much pleased that you and your family were able to accept my invitation," Elizabeth said, hugging her friend.

"Something has changed, Eliza, for you have a glow of contentment about you!" Charlotte noted.

"I noticed the same, Lizzy," Jane agreed. "When we saw you in London you were happy, but this is something new."

"Go change and wash, and I promise that I will talk to you both later," Elizabeth could not help smiling then turned to those who were left to welcome. "Aunt Hattie, are you feeling well?" Elizabeth's aunt was standing rooted to the spot in which she had descended from the carriage, never having imagined that she would see, let alone be guested, in a place such as her niece now called home.

Elizabeth led her aunt into the house. If her aunt was awed at the façade of the house, she was struck dumb at all she saw as her niece led her toward the grand staircase that led to the family floor.

The Bennets, the Gardiners, and the Philips all had suites on the family floor. Bennet did not know it yet, but the enormous suite that he and his wife were shown to by Mrs. Reynolds was just yards from double doors that would lead him to a bibliophile's nirvana.

The rest of the arriving guests were shown to suites on the second floor, the first of the three guest floors. Even with the arrival of eight families, only a small number of the available chambers at Pemberley were occupied. The Long's nieces, who were four and ten and two and ten, respectively, were pleased to be sharing a suite next to their aunt and uncle rather than being placed in the guest floor's nursery.

To the delight of the both the two Gardiner boys and the youngest Lucas son, the latter was placed in the nursery on the family floor with the Gardiners so he would not be alone in the guest nursery.

Elizabeth asked Jane and her betrothed to meet with her and William in their private sitting room after washing and changing from the road.

--*-*-*-*-*-*-*-*-*-*-*

"If we were not so close to your master suite, I would have gotten hopelessly lost, Lizzy," Jane laughed as she seated herself on a comfortable sofa in her sister and brother-in-law's sitting room. Not many minutes later the three were joined by Bingley.

"We asked you to meet us in private as we have a request and want your honest answer without any pressure to grant what we ask," Elizabeth opened.

"Please know that we will hold nothing against you should you feel that you are not inclined to allow what we ask," Darcy backed his wife's words with his own.

"This must be serious!" Jane exclaimed, not being able to imagine what her sister would ask that she would think to deny.

"You both know that our wedding was not exactly a celebration," Elizabeth explained. "We want to know if you two would object if we were to share the ceremony with you. It is our desire to say our vows again when we both mean *every word* in them."

It took Jane a few moments to assimilate what Elizabeth had stressed. While she was thinking, Bingley gave his own verdict. "For my part, I would be honoured to have you share the day with us, as long as my Jane does not object."

"Object! Why would I? Even had this not been at Pemberley, you know that it was always our dream to marry in a double ceremony, Lizzy, and now we shall have that. Of course I want you and William to share the day with us. Lizzy do not toy with me. Did I understand correctly, do you mean *all* the vows?" Both Elizabeth and Darcy nodded, their smiles growing as they agreed.

"Of what are you three talking?" A confused Bingley asked, knowing he was missing something but not sure what.

"They are in love, silly," Jane informed her betrothed.

"Oh...OH! I am so happy for both of you. Now I comprehend why you said what you did, Lizzy. Is it not a great thing, to be in love with the one you are to marry—or in your case are married to?" Bingley said.

"Come, Jane, we need to find Mama and Mrs. Reynolds. It will not mean much of a change. You have an appointment to meet our rector, Mr. Grant Wright, tomorrow He has the livings of Pemberley and Kympton. He will want to see Charles's licence, and we need to inform him of the change to the number of couples," Elizabeth babbled in her excitement. "William, will you please end my father's suspense and show him the library?"

"It will be my pleasure, Elizabeth," Darcy replied sincerely, for he was looking forward to seeing his father-in-law's reaction.

Darcy knocked on the Bennet parents' suite and found his father-in-law studying the volumes in the sitting room bookcase. "Would you like to see where all of their mates reside, Bennet?" Darcy asked.

Bennet became quiet, for he understood perfectly what the not-so-cryptic question meant. "Lead the way, son." They stepped into the hall; Darcy turned left, took ten steps, then stopped at a set of double doors. He pushed the doors open and stepped back as Bennet walked into the largest library he had ever beheld.

He did not have a bed in the library, but he had the next best thing! He could practically roll out of his bed, and he would be in this hallowed hall of books. "It seems that my daughter had us placed in the ideal suite," Bennet stated as he turned around in a circle, awed by what he saw. This was a room he could happily live and die in. With his responsibility of looking after his family, he allowed that he would not spend *all* of his time in this sanctuary, but if he could not be found, it would be easy to guess where he was.

--*-*-*-*-*-*-*-*-*-*-*-*

Jane and Elizabeth asked their mother to join them in Elizabeth's study, where they informed her of the changes to the wedding. "That is a capital idea, Lizzy. Truly you are in love with William?" Fanny asked to reassure herself as the three sat on the sofa within.

"Yes, Mama, I love him with all of my heart," Elizabeth confirmed.

"When did this happen, Lizzy?" her mother asked.

"I am not sure, Mama; I was in the middle before I realised that I had begun. All my prejudices of the past were set aside before we departed London, and I now believe him to be the best of men," Elizabeth glowed.

"In your case, the cart was put before the horse, but it has worked out for the best. It pleases me that my two oldest daughters have found such good matches." Fanny Bennet could not hold her tears back. "I am such a watering pot of late!"

"Mama, is there a reason that you have been tired and cry

easily these last few months?" Jane asked.

"I am well, Jane, very well indeed." Fanny came close to disclosing her state to her daughters, but her agreement with her husband that they inform the family after the quickening stayed her from revealing all.

Elizabeth sought Charlotte out after her meeting with her mother and Jane to inform her best friend of the changes in her feelings for William. Charlotte was understandably relieved on her friend's behalf.

--*-*-*-*-*-*-*-*-*-*-*-*

William Collins found Bennet ensconced in the library and had been granted permission to ask Mary for a courtship. He found Mary sitting in the warmth of the conservatory among the trees and flowers reading her book of sonnets. Mrs. Annesley had agreed to sit just outside the open door to maintain propriety.

"Cousin Mary," Collins called softly. Mary started as she had been lost in what she was reading and had not heard his approach. "I did not mean to startle you. My apologies for disturbing your solitary reverie."

"You have, but it does not follow that said disturbance is unwelcome," Mary blushed becomingly as she pushed her eyeglasses back up her nose.

"I would hope not, Mary. We two have become good friends these months since we met, I think," Collins probed.

"*Just* friends?" Mary asked boldly.

"My hope is that we have become a lot more than simply friends. Mary, I must confess that I have developed tender feelings for you, and with your father's permission, I request the great honour of a courtship with you." Collins was deeply relieved at the look of pleasure that suffused Mary's face.

"I, too, have tender feelings for you, William," Mary admitted. "Yes, I will accept a courtship with you, and with the greatest of pleasure."

"At the risk of disturbing your father as he loses himself in the Darcy's library, I will inform him that you have accepted my offer, Mary," Collins replied excitedly.

"No, William, *we* will go and tell him!" The couple exited the conservatory with Mrs. Annesley trailing behind them as they hurried toward the library. They received many wishes of joy at dinner that night.

One way or another, Longbourn was secure. Either Fanny Bennet carried the heir, or, per his agreement with Mr. Bennet, Collins would change his name to Bennet and Mary would be the mistress of the estate after her father went to his eternal reward.

'I will soon have only two unmarried daughters,' Fanny Bennet marvelled to herself that night. *'God has been exceptionally good to us!'*

CHAPTER 10

The Fitzwilliams, including the newlywed Richard and Anne Fitzwilliam and Lady Catherine, arrived at Pemberley a few days after the large party from Hertfordshire. Thankfully, the Smithtowns were not among the new arrivals, and they were *not* missed!

It was noticeable that Anne Fitzwilliam looked very wan, but the fact was judiciously ignored, and everyone wished the newlyweds well and happy. Richard joined his cousin in the master's study after leaving his wife with Mrs. Jenkinson, who had remained in their employ in the capacity of nurse to Anne.

"The doctor thinks that the end is closer for Anne than we all feared. It is becoming harder and harder for her to breathe normally, and she is fatigued by even a little physical activity," Richard reported.

"Aunt Cat seems to be putting on a brave face," Darcy noted.

"She is, but she is aware of the reality of the situation. I offered Anne the option of remaining at Rosings where it is somewhat warmer than Derbyshire, but she wanted to be here with all of the family around her. She told me that she knows that she will never be able to see Pemberley again." Richard allowed maudlin thoughts to overwhelm him momentarily. He had not made a love match, but that did not mean that he did not care deeply for his wife's wellbeing.

"I have some good news," Darcy changed the subject in an attempt to distract his cousin. "Elizabeth told me that she loves me!"

"You lucky dog!" Richard cheered up some. "How did you

manage to charm your way into your wife's heart? Do not tell me that my taciturn cousin has become a romantic."

"We reached a decision that if we did not attempt to make the best of our lot that we would be condemning ourselves to a life of misery, and, well—one thing led to another, and now we have *both* expressed our love for each other," Darcy beamed with pleasure.

"So...she is your wife in *every* way?" Richard inquired delicately. Darcy had confided in his cousin about his promise not to demand his rights.

"Yes! What about you? I always thought that Anne was too frail for marital relations," Darcy returned Richard's favour of enquiring about indelicate subjects.

"It was not my plan, but Anne wanted to consummate the wedding so she would experience *all* facets of marriage before her illness steals her away from us. I could not refuse her," Richard owned sadly.

"As long as you are catering to her needs and giving her as much happiness as you are able to, she will leave this world having lived her life to the fullest that she was able." This time both men turned maudlin as thoughts of losing Anne could not but be acknowledged.

--*-*-*-*-*-*-*-*-*-*-*

Between all of the ladies in the family, it was decided that the wedding, and the Darcys' renewal vows, would be on Friday the eight and twentieth day of December. Lady Catherine found the organising of said event cathartic as it distracted her from the possibility of losing her only child.

Bingley and Jane would reside at the dower house after the wedding, a structure not much smaller than Longbourn, until the first Friday in January, the day before the Twelfth Night Ball. That would allow the new Mr. and Mrs. Bingley about a sennight of privacy before they joined the rest of the residents of the manor house.

Mr. Wright met with both couples in one of Pemberley's parlours to go over the order of service. Because one was a wedding and the other a renewal, he explained that Mr. Bingley and Miss Bennet would be married first, after which the Darcys would renew their vows. Because of the way the ceremony would be conducted, Darcy and his wife would be able to stand up with Bingley and Jane before they said their vows to one another.

Mr. Wright requested that his patron remain to talk to him when the discussion for the ceremonies was complete. "Mr. Collins has impressed me greatly in the time that he has been in residence at Pemberley. With Mr. Holden's imminent retirement in Lambton, I believe that Mr. Collins would be the ideal candidate to guide the parishioners of that church," Mr. Wright suggested.

"He holds the living in Hunsford next to my cousins' estate," Darcy stated.

"I am aware of that, Mr. Darcy. However, as you know he is courting Miss Mary Bennet. He has shared with me that she would love to live closer to her sister Elizabeth." Mr. Wright waited for his patron to consider his suggestion.

"Yes, I believe he would be a good fit, but before I make him an offer of the living, I need to consult with my cousin, who is Mr. Collins's patron in Kent. If he and his wife agree, I will talk to my wife's cousin about Lambton.

*_*_*_*_*_*_*_*_*_*_*_*_*

"Anne and Richard, are you sure that you do not object if I offer Mr. Collins the Lambton living? I will only speak to him if neither of you are against the move," Darcy reassured his cousins.

Richard looked at his wife for confirmation. "We are sure, William. The value of the living here is almost double that of

Hunsford. We will not hold Mr. Collins back, and I already know who we will offer the living to. Our curate, Mr. Heathe, is well loved by the parishioners and will be an excellent vicar."

Darcy rang for a footman, telling him to ask the mistress, Miss Mary Bennet, and Mr. Collins to join them. Elizabeth had been apprised of her husband's thinking before her sister and cousin arrived, and she was in full agreement with her husband's plan and excited at the prospect of Mary living in the immediate area.

"Collins, I have a proposition for you," Darcy opened. Darcy related the news about Mr. Holden's retirement, Mr. Wright's recommendation, and Mr. and Mrs. Fitzwilliam's agreement, should he accept the living in Lambton.

"You would be but five miles from me, Mary," Elizabeth pointed out to her sister.

"That is my hope, if she agrees to marry me," Collins started to reply.

'You mean when!' Mary said to herself.

"For me, the challenge of a larger parish is attractive, and I, and we, someday, will be close to family. That being said, thank you Darcy, I will gladly accept your offer. For what it means to you, Mr. and Mrs. Fitzwilliam, I heartily endorse Mr. Heathe as my replacement in Kent. He is an excellent clergyman and has been praying for such an opportunity as he is betrothed but did not want to marry until he felt that he could offer his wife more stability," Collins responded.

"You did not ask, Collins, but the living is worth a little under one thousand pounds per annum," Darcy informed him.

"What if I one day inherit Longbourn?" Collins asked.

"We will cross that bridge when we come to it. Bennet is in excellent health, so even if that happened, it would be years in the future," Darcy answered.

"Why would you not inherit Longbourn?" Elizabeth

wanted to know.

"You never know what happens in life," Collins offered in reply. As Mrs. Bennet's pregnancy had not been publicised to the family, Collins did not mention her state to anyone as his cousin had requested. After the meeting, Richard escorted his wife to their chambers to rest, and Mary sought out her mother. The Darcys sought out Georgiana to tell her that they had a solution for Lambton, and Collins went to see his colleague at Pemberley's parsonage to express his gratitude.

"I am so pleased," Georgiana responded when she was informed of the disposition of the Lambton living. "Mary and I have become remarkably close. Having her live in the neighbourhood will be a boon for me."

"They have to marry first, you know! You enjoy spending time with Kitty and Lydia do you not, Gigi?" Elizabeth worried.

"Kitty and I sketch a lot, but Lydia is very quiet, and for the most part keeps to herself in her chambers," Georgiana stated.

Georgiana's observation was valid. Lydia broke her fast in her chambers, though she did join the family for the midday meal and dinner. Elizabeth decided that she needed to enlist Jane's help in drawing Lydia out once again.

*_*_*_*_*_*_*_*_*_*_*_*_*_*_*

Elizabeth knocked on Lydia's bedchamber's door. When Lydia called 'enter' Elizabeth, followed by Jane, Mary, and Kitty, entered her chambers. "Why are you all here?" Lydia asked softly.

"We are worried about you, Lyddie," Jane informed the youngest Bennet. "There is so much to do at Pemberley, and yet but for a meal here and there, we never see you."

Lydia hung her head in shame. "I do not deserve to be with decent people after what I almost did to myself and my family," Lydia replied, as tears fell down her cheeks.

"Lydia, look at me!" Elizabeth tried to cut through her sister's malaise. Slowly Lydia lifted her head, and a pair of tear-filled blue eyes looked back at Elizabeth as Lydia began to sob. "You remember how angry I was when I was forced to marry William, do you not?" Lydia nodded her head. "Do you see the same now? Do I look angry with my husband or like I am not enjoying my married life?"

"N-no, y-you s-seem q-quite h-happy," Lydia managed between sobs.

"Why do you imagine that is, Lyddie? The past did not change, did it?" Elizabeth guided her sister's thoughts by sharing her own situation, smiling sadly when Lydia shook her head as she dried her eyes with Jane's proffered hanky. "So what do you think changed?" Elizabeth asked her sister.

"I know not," Lydia frowned, wondering how she was expected to know this.

"Come now, Lydia, no matter how you used to behave, you were and are intelligent. If Lizzy could not change the past, what changed?" Mary pushed.

"Her attitude?" Lydia ventured.

"That is part of it," Elizabeth agreed warmly. "The bigger part was my accepting that the past is *in* the past, and nothing I do now will change anything that I or anyone else did then. It was a choice, Lyddie." Elizabeth took her sister's hands in her own and said, "In the end it was a simple decision. Did I want to be the author of my own sorrow and live a life of conflict and unhappiness, or was I willing to put the past *behind* me and work toward building a happy present and future. Which do you think I chose?"

"The latter," Lydia acknowledged.

"Yes, but remember this, Lyddie, because if you do not you are doomed to repeat the errors of the past, and then you will be worse off rather than better off. You must learn from the past and acknowledge your mistakes, so you do not repeat them,"

Jane stated. "You have heard Lizzy talk about remembering the past…"

"As that remembrance gives you pleasure. I have," Lydia owned.

"I would add: Learn from the past first, before Lizzy's saying," Mary opined.

"Do you understand what we are telling you, Lyddie?" Jane asked.

"That if I keep moping around as I have been doing, I will keep making myself unhappy so that nothing will change for me. I must determine for myself to learn and make the changes I need to make so that I can be happier?"

"Correct!" Mary encouraged.

"Kitty, do you have anything to add?" Jane asked.

"Just that I owe Lydia and all of you an apology. I am older that Lydia, and rather than try to check her, I followed along and egged her on. I have a lot of lessons to learn from the past and beg not just Lydia's, but all of your forgiveness for the way I used to behave." Kitty met the eyes of each of her sisters as she gave her apology.

"I am so sorry for the way that I used to behave as if I was a spoilt little girl. I cannot believe I was so stupid to fall for all of *that man's* lies!" Lydia remonstrated with herself yet again. "And I am sorry, Kitty, that I used to get you into so much trouble." Lydia hugged Kitty as they both shed tears of regret, both finally coming to terms with their past.

"Lydia, I have an idea. If you four will excuse me, I will be right back." Lydia nodded and the other three Bennet sisters looked on questioningly as Elizabeth turned and exited the chambers.

Elizabeth found Giana reading in her chambers. She told her sister-in-law that she had a favour to ask and explained what she had in mind. Giana agreed without hesitation and the two returned to Lydia's chambers.

"You brought Giana? Does she know what I almost did?" Lydia asked with embarrassment.

"Yes, she does, and she does not judge you for it. Before Giana talks to you, remember that I was taken in by Wickham as well, Lyddie. If I had used my innate good sense, I would have seen all of the contradictions and clear lies in the tale that he spun for me. Like you, I believed what I *wanted* to," Elizabeth pointed out.

"So, there are two of us in the family that he deceived? He most certainly had his fun, did he not?" Lydia asked.

"Three!" Giana exclaimed, and she proceeded to share her story of Ramsgate. "You see, Lydia, with all of my education and advantages I was still taken in by that libertine. We are all better off that he is no longer in this world!" When Giana completed her story of Wickham there was silence.

After a few moments, the four sisters, who had been unaware of Giana's almost ruin, each hugged her. The last to do so was Lydia. The two girls held onto one another tightly, acknowledging membership in a club both would have preferred never to remember.

"If Giana had not told you of her folly, would you have been able to tell that something so disastrous almost befell her?" Elizabeth asked.

"I would not." Lydia took Giana's hand. "May we talk about this later?"

"Anytime you want, we are sisters after all," Giana responded sincerely.

It was at that moment that an unshakeable bond was forged between the two girls. Giana would always be close to Elizabeth, Jane, Mary, and Kitty, but the shared experience of surviving the late George Wickham created a deeper relationship between her and Lydia.

"Sisters, am I forgiven for my past behaviour?" Lydia asked hopefully.

Jane looked to Elizabeth, Mary, and Kitty as each nodded. "We forgive you and Kitty. Now, do you think it is time that you left these chambers and joined us in enjoying our sister's home?"

"Allow me some time to wash and change, and I will join you. Oh, Lizzy, I cannot believe that I have my own maid; thank you very much." For the first time since she realised how close she came to ruin, Lydia started to allow optimism back into her life.

Lydia washed her face and the maid helped her into a warm day dress. When she arrived in the drawing room, she ran to her mother and threw her arms around Fanny Bennet's neck. "I am so sorry for everything, Mama," Lydia whispered into her mother's ear.

"How could I not forgive you, Lyddie. I love all five of you and am much pleased by how much happier you are. At last I have my daughter back," Fanny replied softly as she hugged her youngest fiercely.

"Things will be better with me, Mama, I promise." Bennet, who was not in the library just then, raised his eyebrows in question toward his two oldest daughters.

Jane whispered in her father's ear: "Things will be well with Lydia now. We will tell you what transpired later, Papa."

Lydia threw her energies into joyously decorating the house with greenery in preparation for Christmas that afternoon.

CHAPTER 11

Christmas had come and gone. The residents and guests of Pemberley had enjoyed the festive season immensely. Richard Fitzwilliam was his normal jovial self, always ready with an entertaining story from his days in the army. He seemed to enjoy Kitty Bennet's company, and the two found much to talk about.

The ever-pragmatic Anne Fitzwilliam did not begrudge the time her husband spent speaking with other women. She had no doubt that her remaining time might be weeks or months—not years. She wished him happy as he was making her during the last stages of her life.

"Richard, I need to talk to you," Anne told her husband one night as the two sat in their shared sitting room.

"I will always hear anything you want to say, Anne," Richard replied with no little concern.

"We both know that I do not have much time left, and I want you to make me a promise, Richard," Anne spoke evenly.

"You never know what miracle God may bestow, Anne!" Richard returned. "And I will do anything that is in my power to do for you!"

"Each day it becomes harder for me to draw breath, Richard, so let us not be like children believing some myth that we know impossible. While I do not question the power of God, I can feel my body and I know my time with you will not be long. This trip was important for me to able to say goodbye to my family." Anne got a teasing glint in her eye and added, "At least those I wanted with me."

"My *dear* brother is still in a mood over my inheriting Rosings. If father had not put safeguards in place, he would have frittered away all of Matlock's fortune at the tables, and not just the Smithtown's," Richard lamented.

"I have seen that you enjoy Kitty Bennet's company," Anne held up her hand. "I do not mean to censure you so calm yourself. If she is your choice after I am gone, if she is the one who will make you happy, then know that you have my full and unreserved blessing. Now to the favour. I do not want you to mourn me a year. No more than three months complete!" Anne said with purpose, not acknowledging her own wheezing but hearing it getting harsher.

"How can I mourn my wife for only three months?" Richard reared back as if slapped.

"This afternoon, I met with Mama and your parents. I made my wishes known and listened to each objection they raised, and, in the end, they saw the wisdom in my request. You will have the family's full support in this, Richard," Anne insisted.

"In that case, Anne, I will bow to your wishes," Richard replied. "I can see you are tired; allow me to assist you to you chambers where your maid and Jenkinson await you."

Anne acquiesced, and after he wished his wife a good night, Richard retired to his chambers.

--*-*-*-*-*-*-*-*-*-*-*

On the Thursday after Christmas, Miss Bingley was finally allowed into Scarborough under the watchful eye of one of Aunt Hildebrand's footmen. She made a show of entering several establishments and perusing their wares. By the time she reached the jewellers she had chosen to sell her mother's jewellery, the footman was used to standing near the door waiting for her to leave the shop.

She sold her pieces for over fifty pounds. Although she was aware they were worth more than double that amount, it was enough for her purposes. The next part of her plan was to send the footman on a wild goose chase after she went to the inn for luncheon. Things went her way when she claimed to have left her reticule, an empty one she brought for show, at one of the stores she visited.

She told the flustered servant that she would wait in the dining parlour at the inn until his return. As soon as the man was away, Miss Bingley exited the rear of the inn where a for-hire carriage could be found.

After the first two refused to do business with a lady, the third man was willing. His carriage was old and rickety, but it would do. She agreed to pay the man five and twenty pounds, five times his normal rate, if he would pick her up as instructed and convey her to her destination. She handed him two pounds and told him he would receive the rest at the destination. Although he tried to obtain a five-pound deposit, they settled on three.

When the footman returned with her *lost* reticule, Miss Bingley was drinking tea, waiting where she had said she would be. Her last errand was her brother's local solicitor, who managed her dowry for her traitorous brother. As he had for her other stops, the footman waited outside.

"Did you have an appointment, Miss Bingley?" the solicitor asked as the woman seated herself in his office without invitation.

"Why would I need one when you earn money off the management of my dowry!" she demanded rudely.

"How may I assist you?" the man asked with a sigh of resignation.

"I am here to collect my dowry," Miss Bingley stated in a matter-of-fact manner, as if her request were an everyday occurrence.

"Then I am afraid you have wasted your time today, Miss Bingley. None but your brother may release your dowry." The truth was that Bingley had suspected his sister might attempt to withdraw her dowry, so he had instructed the solicitor to contact him as soon as she tried.

"It is *my* money. You are a thief, and I will report you to the magistrate," Miss Bingley blustered. The money was critical so she would have funds to escape after she made Eliza Bennet suffer.

"If you like, I will happily accompany you to the magistrate with the documents that your brother signed," the man replied coolly.

Miss Bingley knew that she had lost her dowry and stormed out of the office, but only after pushing everything that was on the man's desk onto the floor. The solicitor then quite understood why the shrew's brother had left him the instructions he had.

--*-*-*-*-*-*-*-*-*-*-*-*

"Is it bad news, Charles?" Jane asked as she saw the concern etched on her betrothed's features when he read the missive which had been delivered express.

"You can say that!" Bingley answered. "It is Caroline! Come Jane, we need to speak to Darcy, my sister, and the rest of the family."

Not too long afterwards, they all met in the Darcy's private family sitting room. "What is it, Bingley?" Darcy asked, concerned when he saw how troubled his friend was.

Bingley related what his solicitor had reported. "The only reason that she would attempt to gain control of her dowry is if she hatched some hairbrained scheme that would involve Pemberley, and more than likely is some form of revenge against those she thinks wronged her. If she departed last night by carriage, she will be here Saturday night. She is not a rider and cannot send herself here as an express, so that is her only option," Bingley informed the listeners.

"Where would she get the funds to hire a carriage to transport her?" Bennet frowned.

"Her half of Mama's jewels!" Louisa gasped as the realisation hit her. "If she received even a fraction of their worth, there will be more than enough funds for her purpose."

"If that is the case, the number of footmen and guards on duty at night, no at all times, will be tripled," Darcy stated resolutely.

"This is what I think we should do..." the former colonel laid out a strategy to catch her where she would not be able to claim a misunderstanding. Richard had resigned his commission, but his strategic mind remained with him.

"That is an excellent plan, son," the Earl said proudly.

"We will delay the wedding until the threat is taken care of," Bingley stated with Jane's approval.

"William and I agree," Elizabeth concurred. "Though I hope it will not be delayed too long.

--*-*-*-*-*-*-*-*-*-*-*

The carriage driver was on time and waiting when Miss Bingley slipped out of her aunt's house after midnight, and the coachman informed her that they would make Thorne by that evening. As the way was through hilly terrain, they would overnight there and depart Saturday morning, intending to arrive at their destination Saturday evening.

Having made the trip from Pemberley to Scarborough once already, Miss Bingley was aware that it took two days' travel, so she was not overly concerned that a stop was planned. She knew that her miserable aunt would discover her missing in the morning, but she would think her on the way to Town. That amused her more than it concerned her.

She made herself as comfortable as she could in the old conveyance, counting each minute as it took them farther and farther from Scarborough and her hated aunt.

--*-*-*-*-*-*-*-*-*-*-*-*

The next morning, Miss Hildebrand Bingley did indeed discover her niece was missing and that her bed had not been slept in. Within a half hour, a second express was on its way to Pemberley.

Miss Bingley would not have appreciated the irony, but an express rider with her aunt's missive passed her in the early afternoon.

--*-*-*-*-*-*-*-*-*-*-*-*

The Smithtowns had both been bored at the Viscountess's parents, so the day after Christmas they returned to Town. Lady Jaqueline was soon in the arms of her paramour, and Lord Ulysses decided to visit one of his married lady friends whose husband was purported to be at his country estate. He preferred married paramours; it gave him a sense if power over their husbands.

That night Sir Maxwell Pierson returned to London earlier than he had told his wife he would. Although he did not love, or like, his wife, and had three mistresses in keeping, he was a supremely jealous man and suspected that she had a lover.

He arrived at his town house on Portman Square on Saturday night and heard noises of copulation coming from his wife's chambers as he listened outside the door. He calmly returned to his study and withdrew the case containing his Boutet duelling pistols. He loaded both weapons, cocked them, and returned to his wife's chambers.

Sir Maxwell burst in and shot his wife and the man cuckolding him before they had a chance to separate. He then reloaded one of the pistols. The servants who were drawn by gunfire in the mistress's chambers watched in horror as the master calmly lifted a pistol and shot himself in the head.

--*-*-*-*-*-*-*-*-*-*-*-*

Miss Bingley arrived at the Lambton Inn a little before six

in the evening on Saturday. She paid the coachman the balance she owed, then asked if he would like to earn ten pounds to convey her an additional five miles. He agreed greedily, so they arranged for him to pick her up at midnight.

Miss Bingley rented a room and then walked to the blacksmith's shop. There she purchased a dagger for her *self-protection*. She then decided to rest as she would need her strength when she finally dealt with the chit who had destroyed her dreams, amused that the country nobody knew nothing about what was in store for her that night.

--*-*-*-*-*-*-*-*-*-*-*

"I suspected that she was unhinged, but not to this degree!" Louisa lamented. "To buy a dagger! She intends to murder Lizzy, I am afraid!" The latest reports from the watchers in Lambton had just been revealed.

"Forewarned is forearmed," Elizabeth soothed her friend and soon to be sister.

"It is not that she will come close to succeeding," Bingley stated, "but that she has descended so far. Her greed, pretentions, and delusions have driven her to this."

"It is good that your aunt knew where you would be, so she was able to confirm that Miss Bingley had absconded from her house," Darcy observed.

"My cousin has the right of it, for it was only conjecture after the solicitor's express. The one from your aunt was confirmation. Is everyone clear on their roles tonight if we receive notice that she is, in fact, on her way here?" Richard asked. There was no negative answer.

--*-*-*-*-*-*-*-*-*-*-*

One of Darcy's men watching the insane woman saw the coachman drinking an ale in the taphouse. "Mind if I joins yer fer a pint?" the man asked. "Can I buy ya another one?"

"Don mind if ya does," the coachman agreed, for any coin

not spent was a pleasure to keep for another day's ale. "Ya fr'm 'ere abouts?" His drinking partner nodded. "Ow far is Pember-land fr'm 'ere?"

"Do ya mean Pemberley?" Darcy's man asked.

"Yeah, that be the one," the coachman confirmed.

W'at yer want at Pemberley?" the man prodded.

"Not me, me pass'nger. She wants ta go there. I know not why nor needs to know," The coachman drained his tankard. "Strange bird, wanna go at midnight she does. She pays well, so I goes w'en 'n wear' she wants."

After another ale, the man claimed that he needed to get home to his missus. Minutes later, the intelligence was on its way to the former colonel.

--*-*-*-*-*-*-*-*-*-*-*

Miss Bingley's hired carriage arrived at Pemberley when the clock was approaching quarter to one. "If you wait here for me, there is another five pounds in it for you," Miss Bingley told the man.

"A'right mistress," the coachman shrugged, thinking that he had certainly chosen wisely as no one in their right mind would pay so much for so little, and he was pleased he had let her line his pocket rather than another's. Miss Bingley walked to the side of the house and slipped in through the door that was used for those going and coming from the stables. No sooner had the lady disappeared than three large men and a gentleman of quality confronted the coachman.

"We know you are not party to her plans. Unless you want to be arrested as an accessory, leave now and never return," Bennet told the quaking man. He did not need to be told twice, so with a flick of the reins the vehicle was soon moving back up the drive and off Pemberley's land.

Miss Bingley could not believe her luck! She was climbing the grand staircase, and at least so far, she had seen nary a servant. When she arrived at the landing, she turned left. Having learnt the location of the master suite on her first visit to Pemberley, she knew which door led to what should have been her chambers had Eliza Bennet not stolen it all from her.

She opened the door slowly and saw a form in the bed, outlined by the light of the waning moon. She withdrew the dagger from its sheath and raised it above her head with both hands. "This is what you deserve you whore! Now die!" Miss Bingley cackled as she brought the dagger down with all the force she could muster.

Rather than the satisfying feel of the blade entering her enemy's body, she felt no resistance. Thinking she had missed, Miss Bingley repeated the action a few more times, becoming more and more frustrated when she saw no blood.

Suddenly the chamber was bathed in light as multiple people holding candles walked in. "You have just attempted to murder my wife, Miss Bingley! *Nothing will save you from the gallows now!*" Darcy yelled at her.

When she whirled around in disbelief, she saw her brother, Hurst, Mr. Darcy, Colonel Fitzwilliam, and others she did not know. How could this be? How could Eliza beat her again! Miss Bingley turned and ran before anyone could grab her. "Stop that woman!" Richard commanded.

She got as far as the top of the stairs when a footman grabbed her arm. She pulled with all she had but could not shake him free. Remembering the dagger in her hand, she stabbed wildly towards the man's hand. The dagger found its mark and he released her, but the force she had pulled with sent her tumbling down the grand staircase. When the men reached her at the base of the stairs, she was not moving and was lying face down in a pool of her own blood.

While falling, the dagger had found a target. It was embedded to the hilt in her heart. While Miss Bingley never lived at Pemberley as its mistress, at least she died in the house she coveted.

CHAPTER 12

Miss Bingley's body was carted away in the early hours of Sunday morning. That same day, Bingley and Louisa agreed that they would not allow their late sister's maniacal actions to further delay the wedding.

The ceremony would be Monday morning at eight. Darcy, Hurst, and Bingley met with the magistrate to go over any questions he had about the incident at his offices in Lambton before Miss Bingley's body was buried in the non-consecrated section of the graveyard reserved for criminals in the town.

There had been a debate about whether a mourning period, a short one, should be observed for Miss Bingley. Lady Catherine settled the matter. "If someone we did not know broke into the house and died trying to kill one of us, would we mourn their loss?" she asked pointedly.

"You know we would not, Cat," the Earl replied.

"Then the same should be true here. Did you two," Lady Catherine looked at Bingley and Mrs. Hurst, "not mourn the loss of your sister when she became estranged from you?"

"We did, Lady Catherine," Louisa said thoughtfully.

"You may call me Aunt Catherine tomorrow; you will be a relative after all, though not Aunt *Cat*, as some of my irreverent nephews do," Lady Catherine teased.

"We could call you Aunt Kitty," Elizabeth teased her aunt.

"I believe that I will live with Aunt Catherine, thank you niece," Lady Catherine responded affectionately. "The material point is that in life Miss Bingley caused disruption to your lives;

do not allow her to do so in death."

"That settles it; we will miss who she was before she lost her mind and remember that Caroline has been gone from us for some years already. I have no idea who the insane criminal who attempted to murder Lizzy was, but she was not any sister of mine," Bingley stated with finality.

"How is the footman that was stabbed?" Kitty Bennet asked Elizabeth.

"He is well, Kitty. The doctor said that the wound was superficial so all it needs is some salve and to keep it clean," Elizabeth related happily. She would have hated for anyone to be seriously hurt by the late deranged woman.

--*-*-*-*-*-*-*-*-*-*-*-*

When the Viscountess was informed of her of her husband's manner of death, she was in the arms of her lover, an actor from Drury Lane. Her maid, the only one who had known her location, had no choice but tell the men looking for her where to find her, given the severity of their news.

Lady Jacqueline knew that she would never survive the scandal. Her father would not take her back, the Fitzwilliams would disown her, and even if she were with child and it were to be a male child, it would never be accepted as the heir to the Matlock earldom.

Lady Jaqueline Fitzwilliam did not want to live as a penniless outcast. She had her driver take her to the banks of the Thames. She told him that she desired a walk to clear her head after hearing that her husband was dead, instructing him to return the carriage to Smithtown House.

Once alone, she walked to a nearby bridge. Seeing no one near her, she climbed over the railing and jumped before anyone could reach her. She had decided to take the coward's way out rather than face disgrace. The former viscountess had never learnt to swim so she quickly sank.

Her body was never found.

On Monday morning, the penultimate day of the year 1811, Charles Bingley and Jane Bennet stood before Mr. Wright as he conducted the Church of England's marriage ceremony. With Elizabeth and William Darcy standing up with them and their family, old and new, as well as their friends who had been invited from Meryton as witnesses, Jane Bennet became Jane Bingley.

After the Bingleys signed the register, they returned the favour and stood up for the Darcys as they repeated their vows, this time both meaning every *single* word. When the renewal of vows was complete, everyone wished both couples happy and walked back to the manor house to enjoy a lavish wedding breakfast.

After two hours, the newlywed Bingleys made the one-mile trip to the dower house, where they would be in solitude until the morning of Twelfth Night. As soon as they arrived, they dismissed their personal servants and retired to the master bedchamber.

All of their pent-up passion was relieved as they explored one another's bodies. After quickly divesting each other of clothing, they fell onto the bed. They did not get much sleep that night as Jane discovered the truth of what her married sister had told her about the giving and receiving of pleasure.

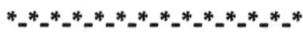

After the wedding breakfast, Collins approached his cousin and requested permission for a private interview with Mary. Bennet, knowing that his cousin and middle daughter were well suited one to the other, granted the request without reservation.

Collins waited in a parlour and Bennet led Mary in. "Ten minutes, Collins. I do not have to tell you that the door will not be closed all the way, do I?" Bennet warned.

Once alone, Collins dropped to one knee. "Mary, I may not have said the words to you, but I hope that you know that I love you."

"I do, William, and I love you in return," Mary replied, glowing with happiness.

"Rather than spout flowery words from one of the Bard's sonnets, I will speak plainly. I love you for your mind, you compassion, and your charity. There is none other I could imagine as my partner in life. Mary Patricia Bennet, will you please accept my hand in marriage and be my wife?" Collins asked as he looked up in the eyes of the woman that he loved.

"For some time I have been dreaming of the day when you would ask this question, and my answer has been ready since my first daydream. It is yes, William, absolutely and irrevocably yes!" Mary responded as Collins stood. He kissed his betrothed softly and both felt a wave of pleasure that shook them to their cores.

Wisely, they stepped back from one another as there was a knock on the door, followed by Mr. and Mrs. Bennet. Permission was canvassed and granted without delay. After congratulating her middle daughter and soon to be third son, Fanny Bennet exclaimed: "I will have three daughters married. God has been exceptionally good to us, Thomas, exceptionally good indeed!"

"So it would seem, Fanny," Bennet agreed.

"Ooooh Thomas, I just felt it!" Fanny exclaimed excitedly.

"The quickening?" Bennet confirmed.

"Yes, Thomas, I felt the quickening!" Fanny was glowing.

"Mama, are you with child?" Mary asked astounded. "How is that none of knew?"

"I am, Mary, yes. Your father told your betrothed as it may impact his future inheritance. Do not look at him so; your father swore him to silence," Fanny reassured her middle daughter.

"In that case, I suppose I will have to forgive him," Mary

smiled at her betrothed and he was relieved not to have angered her.

When the dual blessings were announced, they were met with pleasure and many congratulations. The celebration lasted late into the night, but Jane and Charles Bingley were not disturbed by anyone bringing the latest good news to the dower house.

--*-*-*-*-*-*-*-*-*-*-*-*

On Tuesday afternoon that a rider thundered down the drive toward the manor house at Pemberley. He handed a missive to the butler, who brought it to the drawing room, where all but the newlyweds had congregated. With a bow, the butler handed the black-edged missive to the Earl.

"Ulysses!" Lady Elaine exclaimed. The rest of the family was present, so there were no other options.

"Both of them," Lord Matlock said, stunned. Richard quickly took the missive from his father just as it was about to drop from his hand, discovering that it had been written by their solicitor in Town. He looked to his father, who nodded for him to read the missive aloud.

"It is dated yesterday. I will summarise it, as there is information that may be upsetting to some," Richard stated.

"No Son, read it. The truth is already all over society. Your late brother and sister-in-law have finally caused a scandal for us, even if it is in death." Lord Matlock seemed to age before their eyes as his wife sat next to him and hugged him close.

Richard began to read:

It grieves me to inform you that Viscount Smithtown has been shot. Sir Maxwell Pierson discovered your son in bed with his wife. He shot them both and then himself.

When the Viscountess was informed, she was discovered in the bed of an actor on Drury Lane. She threw herself into the Thames, and her body has not been recovered as of the writing of this missive.

The Countess sobbed into her husband's chest while the rest were silent. What could be said at a time like this? It was Lady Catherine who took charge. "We will *all* depart for Town in the morning. We will show our faces and hold our heads high, and I dare *anyone* to tar any of the rest of us with the same brush as those two. We will call on all of our true friends to stand with us, and we *shall* overcome this!"

"Mama, am I a viscountess now?" Anne asked softly.

"Yes, niece, you are," her uncle responded. "Richard is Viscount Smithtown."

"It seems we have a new Lady Anne in the family," Lady Catherine pointed out.

With Elizabeth's assistance, Lady Catherine helped organise everything for an early morning departure for London. Darcy rode his horse to the dower house to inform the newlyweds of their plans.

Jane and Bingley met Darcy in the drawing room, where he quickly informed them of the events surrounding the death of the Viscount and Viscountess. "Should we come to Town as well?" Bingley asked.

"No, Bingley, there is no need, though I would appreciate it if you and the Hursts would stay here until we return from London. The Bennets and the rest of their family and friends will depart as originally planned with our father-in-law dropping Lydia at school, also as planned," Darcy laid out for the Bingleys. "Giana is staying here, so having you, Jane, and the Hursts with here will be a great relief for me."

"You know you can count on us, Darcy; we are brothers now after all," Bingley smiled.

"We depart in the morning, so if you would like one more night of privacy here, it is yours. I am sure that if you want more than one night, the Hursts will be able to entertain my sister for a few more days," Darcy suggested.

"That will not be necessary; we will move back to the main house today," Bingley stated after he had received a nod from Jane. "We will use the chambers I usually reside in when I visit you."

"No, actually, you have a suite in the family wing, as do the Hursts. You are family now, Bingley. Elizabeth placed you in the Rose suite, as she knows how much your wife likes roses," Darcy informed the newlyweds.

"My sister knows me well," Jane smiled sweetly in appreciation of the thought.

"I will take my leave of you and see you when you return to the manor house." Darcy shook his new brother's hand and gave Jane a peck on the cheek. Bingley's comment of being a brother reminded him of the news shared the night before. "We will soon be three brothers. Collins proposed to Mary, and she accepted him."

"Mary will be very happy with our cousin," Jane gushed.

Darcy departed soon after and rode his horse back to the stables. He entered the house by the same door that Miss Bingley used to infiltrate the mansion and attempt her maniacal attack.

--*-*-*-*-*-*-*-*-*-*-*

"How do you feel now that you outrank your mother?" Lady Catherine teased her daughter. Everyone was sitting in the drawing room after dinner, and she and Anne were in a corner away from the rest.

"Mother, I have a suggestion," Anne said quietly so only her mother could hear.

"What is it, Anne?" Lady Catherine asked intrigued for her daughter had a mind more active than she had ever credited.

"Now that Richard is the Viscount, I have been considering what will become of Rosings. I know that my late cousin all but gutted both Smithtown and Smithtown House in Town. I know that Uncle Reggie has more than enough wealth to repair the damage that his son wrought, but what if he did not need to?" Anne asked.

"Of what are you thinking, Anne? I can see that you have a solution," Lady Catherine asked.

"Rosings is not entailed in any way, is it Mama?" Lady Catherine nodded her head. "Mama, I know that you had a most unhappy marriage. When I pass, the de Bourgh bloodline will die with me." Lady Catherine wiped some tears away as Anne spoke about her impending death. "I know that you were always worried about security, but you have no need to. Do you not see how much you are loved by your family, that you will *never* be alone? I want to sell Rosings, Mama. I will not do it unless you agree, and we have made sure that you will always have a good place to live. The money will restore both the estate and town home, and there will be enough left over to buy a medium sized estate so that if Richard remarries and has sons, his second son will have an estate as well."

"Anne, you are too good! It seems a sound plan, but will you mind if I think on it for a few days? I promise to give you my answer in London." Lady Catherine leaned toward her precious daughter and enfolded her in a hug.

--*-*-*-*-*-*-*-*-*-*-*-*

"William, I will miss you," Mary Bennet told her betrothed as he prepared to depart just before the group travelling to London. His brother-in-law to be had lent him one of his comfortable travel coaches to make the round trip to Hunsford via Meryton.

"I will miss you, Mary, but I have to help the curate transition to his new position and pack up my house. My soon-to-be brother Darcy has offered that we may reside at Pemberley until Mr. Holden leaves at the end of the month. I do not want to hover over him and have him feel like I am pushing him out before he is ready to depart," Collins informed his betrothed.

"Travel safely, William. I will look forward to seeing you

in Meryton for our wedding," Mary blushed at the mention of the ceremony that would take place on the two and twentieth of January. The wedding would be on a Wednesday, which would allow them to be back at Pemberley the Saturday after.

Mary stood and waved until she could no longer see the conveyance bearing her betrothed back to Kent. A half hour later, the train of coaches heading for London departed.

*_*_*_*_*_*_*_*_*_*_*_*_*

No one had noticed, given the events at Pemberley, that Charlotte Lucas had been courted quietly by Mr. Wright, the man who held the livings of Kympton and Pemberley. He was five and thirty, and she seven and twenty, and both were of a practical bent.

Sir William was caught off guard when Mr. Wright approached him the day before the Lucas's departure to request Charlotte's hand in marriage. Once the couple explained to him and Lady Lucas that they had grown to esteem and respect one another over the weeks that Charlotte had been at Pemberley and that they found that they fit one another perfectly, Sir William bestowed his consent and blessing. Mr. Wright would travel to Meryton the week after the group from that neighbourhood departed, for his curate would not be available until then.

The plan was to obtain a common licence in Meryton and then return to the Pemberley parsonage as man and wife. Charlotte sat down to write a letter to Eliza, for she had been very coy and neither Eliza nor Jane had any idea that she was being courted under their noses. At least she would be able to talk to the new Mrs. Bingley before she departed with her parents and family.

CHAPTER 13

Rather than open de Bourgh House, Lady Catherine, Lady Anne, and Lord Richard, the new Viscount, accepted an invitation to join the Earl and Countess at Matlock House. Anne rested in her chambers as everyone else met in the family sitting room to strategize. The Darcys arrived a few minutes earlier from their town home opposite the Earl's.

"I have sent notes to all of our friends, inviting them to dinner on the morrow," the Countess informed the family.

"I wrote to my friends also," Darcy reported. "If there is room, we can all join you for dinner on the morrow and formulate one coherent plan."

"Just let me know how many, William. Thank you for your support," his Aunt replied.

"As if we would not support you! Aunt Cat's plan is sound, and once we are seen in society with our friends around us, no one will dare utter a derogatory word against any of us," Darcy replied, and Elizabeth nodded her complete agreement.

"It does not hurt that Countess de Lieven, Countess Esternhazy, Lady Jersey, and Lady Cowper are all close friends of mine. When we are seen with all four Almack's patronesses, the family of any debutante who wants a voucher again will be silenced," the Countess pointed out.

"It will be well; I just know it," Lady Catherine opined. "Besides, you know I am *never* wrong!" Her family was not yet used to her using self-deprecating humour and laughed like it was a fresh pleasure enjoyed.

"What of Ulysses' body?" Darcy asked.

"It should be back at Matlock by now. It will be kept in the coldest room possible, and we will return in a sennight. There is nothing for it; we must counteract the scandal my late son caused. The future of the family depends on it," the Earl stated firmly.

The ladies all decided that a few dyed older dresses would suffice; they would not be seen at the mantua maker at a time such as this.

--*-*-*-*-*-*-*-*-*-*-*-*-*

A little later, Ladies Catherine and Elaine were sitting together while the rest of the family was busy elsewhere. "I am going to miss her so much, Elaine," Lady Catherine stated sadly. "I am thankful that Anne has had a full life and even became a viscountess before being taken from us. I regret all the time I wasted harassing her and William to marry. I could have used my time far more judiciously rather than trying to order the lives of others," Lady Catherine lamented to her sister.

"Catherine, as much as we would all prefer not to have made mistakes in the past, we all do, and there is naught that we can do to repair them. What is done is done. Spend every moment you are able to with Anne. She knows that you love her and always have," Lady Elaine held her sister's hand. "Richard and Reggie are deciding which funds to use to repair the mess that Ulysses made of the town house and the estate."

"There is no need to use Matlock funds. Anne had an idea, and I agree with her. It is sound." Lady Catherine proceeded to inform her sister what their daughter Anne had decided, and the ladies agreed that they needed to inform the Earl and the new Viscount.

When Lady Catherine informed her son-in-law and brother that she agreed with Anne, that Rosings Park should be sold to restore the damage wrought by the late viscount, as well as providing funds to purchase a medium sized estate for a second son, the two men were flabbergasted.

"Are you and Anne sure?" the Earl asked once he found his voice.

"We are. Richard actually owns Rosings now as Anne's husband, but he has been gracious enough to defer in matters regarding the disposition of the estate to my Anne while she is still with us. It is her dearest wish to do this. She is correct; there are no more de Bourghs by blood after her, other than some of my late husband's by-blows, who may not inherit. Given the contentious relationship I had with Lewis, I have no emotional tie to the estate as long as someone takes me in," Lady Catherine teased, knowing full well that De Bourgh House was hers if she wanted her independence.

"You will live with us, Cat," her brother said after an enthusiastic nod from his wife.

"I am sure that William and Lizzy will welcome you for as long as you want to live with them as well," Lady Elaine stated. "In fact, we may have to argue with them to have any time with you at our residence, for your niece is very fond of you, as we are."

--*-*-*-*-*-*-*-*-*-*-*-*-*

Once they had arrived at Longbourn to allow Fanny, Mary, Kitty, and Lydia to settle at home, Bennet called Lydia into his study before they were to depart for the Wrightfield School for Young Ladies in Wiltshire. "Lydia, if you would like me to find a school closer to home or in Town, I am willing to do so. The changes that you have made so far have impressed me greatly," Bennet told his youngest.

"As much as I appreciate your confidence in me, Papa, I need to go to that school for at least one year. I am learning, but I still have far to go," When she denied his suggestion, Bennet was impressed with the level of self-awareness his daughter was displaying. "I was speaking to William, Mary's William not Lizzy's, and he explained how structured the school is and how they value discipline. At the end of the school year, we can revisit this subject again if you approve," Lydia answered. Bennet kissed his daughter's forehead affectionately as she was dismissed.

He could not believe how much his boisterous younger daughter had matured. The next morning, after many tearful goodbyes, most tears being shed by his pregnant wife, Bennet and his youngest boarded the coach and began the journey to Wiltshire.

--*-*-*-*-*-*-*-*-*-*-*

In addition to the family, the dinner at Matlock House was attended by two dukes and their duchesses, seven earls and countesses, a baron, several baronets, and some very influential non-titled members of the first circles. There was full-throated support for the family, and those present agreed to recruit many of their friends to assist in killing any gossip.

On the morrow, Ladies Elaine, Catherine, and Anne would be seen taking tea at Gunter's with the four patronesses of Almacks and two duchesses, while the high-ranking men would accompany Lords Matlock and Hilldale to Whites. Mr. Darcy intended to join them there. Once the family was seen at one or two public venues with the full support of so many influential members of the Ton, there would be little doubt left about the wisdom of gossiping about the Fitzwilliams.

After the last of the guests had departed, the members of the family were seated in the family sitting room at Matlock House. "That could not have gone better," Lady Catherine opined.

"Cat has the right of it," her brother agreed.

"I mourn the man my son could have been, not the one he ended up being," Lady Elaine agreed sadly.

"We will fix the mess he left us, and then we will go on with life. Here's to the new Viscount Hilldale." Lord Matlock raised his snifter of brandy to his son as the others echoed the sentiment.

"Let us not forget that we have a viscountess in Anne that we actually like," Lady Elaine reminded her family.

Elizabeth noticed that Anne looked white in the extreme. "Anne, are you well?" Elizabeth asked.

"I am just tired," Anne hedged.

Richard stood and helped his wife, who was unsteady on her feet. He scooped her up in his arms and carried her to her bed-chamber so Mrs. Jenkinson and her lady's maid could care for their mistress.

"I think that after we have been seen tomorrow that Anne and I need to retire to Rosings. I know that the travel was necessary, but I think it has been too much for her. I apologise, Mother and Father, but I need to remain with Anne so I will be unable to attend my brother's funeral," Richard stated after he returned to the sitting room.

"My place is at Rosings with Anne and Richard," Lady Catherine insisted.

"Of course, we understand," Lady Elaine responded.

"We will attend the funeral and then return to Pemberley," Darcy stated after conferring with Elizabeth. After making sure they were not needed, the Darcys wished their family goodnight and returned to Darcy House.

The strategy worked just as predicted. Once any who had considered trying to tar all of the Fitzwilliams with the same brush as the former Smithtowns saw the massive show of support, which even had the Queen making positive comments about the surviving Fitzwilliams, the scandal became a non-event. There were none who wanted to run afoul of so many leading voices of the Ton.

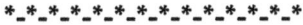

After the funeral, the Darcys returned to Pemberley, where they found a happy Georgiana and an excited Jane and Bingley. "Darcy, do you know Ashford Dale?" Bingley asked as soon as Darcy and Elizabeth joined them in the drawing room after changing.

"Yes, I know it well; it is just the other side of Lambton, not ten miles from Pemberley. Why do you ask?" Darcy responded.

"It *was* for sale. The Ashfords decided to move to the New World and had the estate up for an extremely reasonable price. They want to leave as soon as may be to join the rest of their family in the former colonies, a place called Virginia, I think," Bingley related.

"If you purchase it, you will be so close to us," Elizabeth said enthusiastically.

"Do not forget that Mary and William will be between us in Lambton," Jane reminded her sister.

"It is not an if," Bingley grinned, "the price was excellent for an estate that brings in five thousand five hundred clear, so I purchased it. You are looked at the master and mistress of Ashford Dale. The sale was final yesterday," Bingley reported proudly.

"The last time I heard, it was a very sound estate," Darcy stated. "It will be most pleasant to have our brother and sister just over an hour away by carriage, even closer by horseback."

"Charles wrote to Uncle Philips to notify him that we will not be renewing the lease on Netherfield," Jane reported.

"Will Mama not be distraught with you leaving the neighbourhood too?" Elizabeth asked.

"No, Mama and Papa looked over the estate with us before they departed, and they agree that it is perfect for us. Mama will have a new baby to keep her busy in four or five months, and Papa said they will just have to visit more often so he will be able to make sure all is well with William's library," Jane reassured her sister.

"When Mr. Collins and Mary move to Pemberley before Mr. Holden's retirement, how will we know which William is being addressed when both brother and Mr. Collins are in the same room?" Georgiana asked.

"That is a quandary, Giana. We will have to find a solution

before we leave for the wedding," Darcy chuckled. "We have a few days before we depart for Longbourn to think of one."

"Is not the simplest solution to call you Darcy and him Collins when you are both in the same room?" Elizabeth suggested. The other four agreed it was as good a solution as any other. Elizabeth would suggest it to Mary when they saw her the day before her wedding.

--*-*-*-*-*-*-*-*-*-*-*

Bennet had no sooner entered the house when his wife pounced. "How is my baby? Is she settled? Will she be lonely? Will she not be homesick?" Fanny Bennet prattled away, reminiscent of one of her former attacks of nerves.

Bennet understood why. His wife was concerned for Lydia. "She is well, Fanny, I promise you. More than that, she is happy. She has already made friends with her two chamber mates, and she will thrive at the school."

"Lydia's behaviour has improved so much; did she really need to go to this school?" Fanny pushed.

"It was her choice, Fanny! Before we departed Longbourn I gave her the choice to remain here and asked if she would prefer a school closer to home. For well thought out and logical reasons, *she* asked me to give her at least one year at the school," Bennet told his wife.

"If it is her choice, then I will respect it," Fanny settled. After Mary married, it would just be Kitty at home until she left as well, to attend her art school in London.

Bennet understood the thrust of his wife's thoughts. "Before you know it, you will have a babe in arms. Do not forget, Fanny, that Kitty and Lydia will not be at school forever."

"That is true. Excuse me Thomas, you know I become maudlin when I am with child," Fanny replied.

"I well remember, Fanny, and there is naught to excuse you for," Bennet replied affectionately. "Besides, do you not have a wedding to plan?"

"I most certainly do. Mary, **Mary**! Now where is that daughter of yours? We need to plan," Fanny was diverted from her sadness just as her husband expected.

The time passed swiftly, and Collins returned as promised a week before the wedding. He was a guest of Netherfield so that he was not residing in the same house with his betrothed. He was not there alone for long, as he was joined by the Gardiners a day later, and then the Darcys and Bingleys arrived a day before the wedding. Bennet collected Lydia from her school and returned with his youngest the day before as well.

To say that Fanny was happy to see her youngest looking so happy would have been an understatement. After talking to Lydia and hearing that she was enjoying the challenge of her lessons, even given the rigid structure of the school, and was making some friends among the girls, any feelings of residual regret that her mother felt at her daughter being far away dissipated.

Fanny Bennet's talk to Mary the night prior to her wedding was much more positive than the talk she gave her second daughter before her forced marriage. After her mother had given her *the talk*, Mary requested that Elizabeth and Jane attend her in her bedchamber.

Mary related the gist of what her mother had told her and asked her sisters if there was anything that they wanted to add or correct. "No Mary, what Mama has told you will stand you in good stead. I would only add the same that I related to Jane. Never be afraid of taking or giving pleasure. Like I love my William, and Jane loves Charles, you love your William, so whatever you decide pleases you together will never be wrong," Elizabeth reassured her sister.

"Elizabeth's advice to me before my wedding was very useful," Jane informed her sister.

"Thank you, both of you. Given what you and mother shared with me, I find that rather than feeling fear, I am in anticipation," Mary admitted as she blushed scarlet. The sisters hugged, then Elizabeth and Jane kissed Mary on each cheek and left their sister to her thoughts.

--*-*-*-*-*-*-*-*-*-*-*-*

Collins was entertained at Netherfield by Darcy, Bingley, and Bennet. The men playfully warned him that they would be keeping their eye on him, and to always treat Mary well. Darcy and Bingley also ribbed the groom by asking if he needed any advice for the wedding night, which Collins politely refused, much to Bennet's relief.

The only regret that Collins had was that the aunt and uncle who raised him had been unable to attend the wedding, as their youngest had taken ill. He had spoken to Mary, and they would journey to Wiltshire in the spring to spend some weeks with his surrogate parents. She seemed to be looking forward to meeting them as much as he was sure that they would be looking forward to meeting her.

--*-*-*-*-*-*-*-*-*-*-*-*

Bingley stood up for Collins while Kitty did the honours for Mary. Longbourn's rector conducted the Church of England's matrimonial ritual. Not long after the couple said their vows, the clergyman intoned the final benediction. Mr. and Mrs. Collins signed the register, making their union official both in the eyes of God and man.

After hugs and handshakes and with many wishes for joy from the family, they all made the short walk back to Longbourn for the wedding breakfast. It was attended by most of the four and twenty families of the neighbourhood. About two hours later, Mary, with Kitty and Lydia's aid, changed into her travel clothes.

Not long after, followed by some teary goodbyes, hugs, and kisses, the newlyweds boarded the Darcy carriage that Collins had been using to begin their journey to Pemberley. As a gift to the Collins', Darcy arranged their stays at the two inns he used on the Great North Road and made sure the landlords knew to have their biggest and best suites available for these special guests.

It can be safely assumed that Mary and her husband had nothing to repine after their wedding night.

*_*_*_*_*_*_*_*_*_*_*_*_*_*

The Darcys were planning to return to Pemberley the Monday after the wedding, while the Bingleys remained to pack up their belongings at Netherfield. The Darcys' plans changed on Friday when an express was received from Richard, summoning them to Rosings as soon as was possible.

CHAPTER 14

"It is Anne," Richard informed the Darcys. He had been waiting under the portico for them since being informed that the carriage had passed the gatehouse.

"Is she…" Elizabeth began to ask, relieved that there were no black wreaths on the doors.

"No, she still lives, but it will be but hours, or days at best. She has difficulty drawing breath now," Richard explained to his cousins as they handed their outerwear to the new, much younger, butler. "Her mother is with her; she hardly sleeps or does anything other than sit with Anne. The doctor is in residence as well, and as much as he would like to help, other than to make Anne comfortable there is nothing to be done for my wife." Richard's voice cracked as he said the last. It had not been a love match, but he cared deeply for Anne as he had always loved her as a cousin.

"I assume you notified your parents?" Darcy asked.

"Yes," Richard confirmed. "I expect them in the next day or two. I know Anne told me that she said goodbye to everyone at Christmastide, but I know that my Mother and Father would like to see her and say goodbye to her again. I pray that they arrive in time. Go change and then come to the master suite."

A half hour later, the Darcys knocked on Anne's bedchamber door lightly and Mrs. Jenkinson admitted them. There was no mistaking that Anne's long-time companion turned nurse had shed tears. "Miss Anne will be happy that you are here," she said softly as she closed the door.

Anne was in the bed, and while she had always been a slight, frail woman, she seemed to have shrunk even more and her pallor was a creamy white. Richard was sitting on one side of the bed holding her hand while her mother sat on the other side holding her other hand. Although Elizabeth and Darcy approached the bed quietly, Anne opened her eyes halfway as she recognised them.

"You...came," she rasped, and Darcy winced at hearing how hard it was for her to speak.

"Of course we came, Anne," Elizabeth soothed as she pulled up a chair and sat next to Lady Catherine, taking that lady's free hand in her own.

"Oh, Elizabeth," Lady Catherine started but was overcome with tears. Elizabeth leaned over and gave her aunt a warm hug.

"You will *never* be alone," Elizabeth whispered their promise into the older lady's ear. "We will need you as a grandmother!"

It took a minute for the significance of what Elizabeth said to sink in, for at first Lady Catherine misunderstood what Elizabeth was telling her, then her whole expression changed. "Are you with child, Lizzy?" Lady Catherine asked quietly.

"No, Aunt Cat, I am talking about our future children, if we are granted any," Elizabeth clarified.

On the other side of the bed, Darcy sat down next to his cousin. He reached out and brushed his hand against Anne's cheek, sad that was cold to the touch. "Anne, we will miss you, but soon you will be in no more pain," Darcy said quietly as he leaned forward placing his lips near Anne's ear.

"Look...after...him!" Anne's eyes flicked to Richard and Darcy nodded, for she had already told him that she did not want Richard to descend into melancholy after she was gone. At Pemberley she had reiterated their agreement with Richard that he not mourn for more than three months and that he move on, yet she had still made him promise to make sure that Richard did.

She had been concerned that he would feel too guilty to take another wife, which would lead to the end of the Fitzwilliam line, not just the de Bourgh line.

"You have my most solemn promise, Anne," Darcy swore as he leaned further forward and kissed her forehead.

It seemed that Anne had been holding on just to hear Darcy reaffirm his promise. She was calm as she took one more rasping breath, and then she was still. Lady Anne de Bourgh-Fitzwilliam, Viscountess Smithtown, was at peace.

Elizabeth held Lady Catherine in her arms as the mother wept inconsolably for the loss of her daughter. Although silently, Richard too shed some tears as the doctor confirmed what they all knew. Their Anne was no longer in the mortal world.

--*-*-*-*-*-*-*-*-*-*

A day after Anne's passing, when the Matlock carriage approached the entrance to Rosings Park, they knew they had missed saying another goodbye to their niece and daughter-in-law. There was no mistaking the black cloth hanging from the gate posts.

Darcy was waiting for them when their carriage drew to a halt. "How is Richard, William?" his concerned mother asked.

"As well as can be expected. He is sad, but he also is relieved that Anne is no longer suffering, which gives him a measure of comfort. However, Aunt Cat has been inconsolable; Elizabeth has not left her side," Darcy reported.

"It does not matter how long she has known this outcome inevitable; she is a mother who has lost a child and is experiencing the hardest thing a parent can endure," Lord Matlock stated sadly. He was experiencing some measure of guilt that he did not feel much sorrow over his eldest's passing; all he felt was regret for his son's wasted life.

"I believe your presence here will be a boon to my aunt," Darcy opined, addressing both his aunt and uncle. "Since Anne's passing, she has been asking for you two repeatedly."

The Earl and Countess changed and returned to the drawing room. On seeing her brother, Lady Catherine was enfolded in his welcoming arms. "My Anne is gone, Reggie. It is hard for me to accept. Each time I hear someone approach, I look up hoping that it will be Anne," Lady Catherine admitted as she cried on her brother's shoulder.

"Catherine, if you want to change your mind and not sell Rosings, we will understand. If you keep your resolution, then you have a home with us for as long as you live," Lord Matlock soothed his sister.

"Aunt Cat, you know the same is true for us. Elizabeth already invited you to live with us, and I second that invitation as does Giana," Darcy told his aunt emphatically.

"After all... the trouble... I... used to be," Lady Catherine managed between sobs, "you want me to come live with you?"

"YES!" The resounding answer was given by a chorus of five voices.

"And if any of them grate on your nerves, Aunt Cat, know that you will always have a bedchamber ready for you in any of my homes!" Richard added meaningfully.

"I will honour Anne's wishes; we will sell Rosings. Just after she died, I asked myself how I could stand by and see the home where Anne lived sold, but I realised my memories of Anne will always be with me, *wherever* I happen to reside. And besides," Lady Catherine gave a weak smile," Elizabeth has invited me to be a grandmama to the future Darcy children, and I cannot disappoint my favourite married niece."

"I am your *only* married niece, Aunt Cat," Elizabeth returned.

"Lizzy are you..." Lady Elaine stopped herself as there was a maiden in the room.

"No, I am not, Aunt Elaine. As Aunt Cat said, I asked for our *future* children, and, as far as I know, none are on the way." Elizabeth laughed as her husband started to beam and was instantly deflated as she clarified the situation.

Given that Rosings was to be sold, the family decided to transport Anne's body to Matlock and bury her where her mother and family would be able to visit her. The procession departed Rosings Park on the final Tuesday of January and arrived at Matlock on Thursday, the penultimate day of that month.

With the men of the family as well as many friends attending, Anne entered her eternal resting place next to generations of Fitzwilliams who had come before her. A few days after the guests departed, the Darcys prepared to leave Matlock with a new member of their household. Lady Catherine had become much attached to Elizabeth and had elected to make Pemberley her primary home.

Although her nephew and nieces beseeched her to remain at the manor house, Lady Catherine elected to live in the dower house. She could see her family whenever she desired, but she had the level of independence that she enjoyed.

Within a month after Anne was laid to rest, Rosings Park was sold to a wealthy tradesman, who paid a premium as there had been a bidding war to acquire such an estate. There was only one condition of the sale, and the new owner had no objection to it, which was to retain all of the servants from the steward and housekeeper down unless they chose to leave.

The funds were used exactly as Anne wanted. Smithtown House in London and the estate in Staffordshire were returned to their former glory. Some of the tenants that the previous viscount had lost due to his habit of continually raising rents while not attending to their needs, returned to reasonable rents and fully-repaired cottages and farms. The rest of the tenant farms filled rapidly once word was spread that the new master bore no resemblance to his brother.

The final piece of Anne's request was filled when Richard purchased the estate of Glenmeade in the same shire as Smithtown, but twenty miles distant. It would be a perfect estate for a second son, with an income in excess of five thousand per annum.

--*-*-*-*-*-*-*-*-*-*-*

May 1812

"William, I have something to tell you," Elizabeth stated one morning after returning from using the chamber pot behind the screen as she watched her husband lying lazily in their bed staring at her intently.

"What is it, Elizabeth?" he asked his curiosity piqued.

"Have you not noticed that I have not been afflicted with my monthly indisposition for the last few months?" she asked, swaying her hips side to side languidly as he so enjoyed when watching her walk to him.

"I did indeed notice that. Do you really think I would not notice that we did not have to refrain from joining for a week at a time?" Darcy grinned. "I also knew that when you were ready to discuss it with me you would."

"Based on what my mother and Aunt Cat have told me, I believe that I am with child, but we need to have it confirmed by a doctor," Elizabeth informed her husband.

"We can make a stop in London on the way to Netherfield, my love. There are some fine accoucheurs in Town. I will write to one. I believe Mr. Isaac Ashcroft is reputed to be the best. Only the best for my Elizabeth." Darcy suggested.

He had purchased Netherfield from Mr. Morris as a gift for his wife, so they and the rest of their expanding family would always have a place to stay when visiting the area and Longbourn had no more room available.

Darcy pulled his naked wife toward him to kiss her, causing her to giggle. He captured her lips with his own, making her quite forget her mirth, and proceeded to show her what a kiss from a man violently in love with his wife felt like. It was slow and deep, soft, and stirringly thorough; Elizabeth felt her body ache for him all the way to the pit of her stomach, where she believed she was carrying the next generation of Darcys.

When they broke apart for air, Elizabeth looked at her husband saucily. "Is this not what led to my being in this state in the first place?" she teased.

"Minx!" was his only response as he pulled his wife below him and proceeded to love her thoroughly and completely.

--*-*-*-*-*-*-*-*-*-*-*

Elizabeth and Darcy arrived in the breakfast parlour somewhat later than was their wont to find Richard and Lady Catherine both present. "Excuse our tardiness family, we, err, were otherwise engaged," Darcy stated proudly.

"I am sure you were!" Richard exclaimed. Thankfully, Richard was almost back to his jovial self and had just come out of half mourning for Anne, honouring her *no more than three months' of mourning* request.

"Do you not have your own food to eat, *My Lord!*" Darcy mocked playfully.

"Perhaps you should talk to your wife more, William; she invited me," Richard retorted. As he finished speaking, the Collinses and Bingleys were shown in.

After a round of "Jane, Lizzy, Mary" was completed as the sisters greeted one another, the arriving couples helped themselves to some of the abundant food on the sideboard and sat.

"We are all travelling to Netherfield to be there when Fanny enters her final confinement, are we not?" Lady Catherine asked. Surprisingly, she and the Bennet matriarch had become close over the past months, and their correspondence was weekly, or even more frequently if something amusing occurred at one estate or the other. Lady Catherine was in half-mourning as her daughter had not extracted the same promise for her to mourn no more than three months as she had from her husband. She missed Anne every day, but surrounded with love and company as she was, she was doing far better than she would have imagined. Her brother and sister-in-law had completed their mourning, as they had decided to mourn only three months, and in that she also supported their decision for it was far more than they had done for their own son. She was grateful her daughter had been genuinely loved by all.

"Elizabeth and I will take the London turnoff and should arrive a day or two later," Darcy reported nonchalantly.

All eyes turned towards the beaming Darcys. "Why would you be going to London when the rising temperature creates awful odours?" Lady Catherine asked.

"For a meeting," Elizabeth responded. "Are there any needs in your parish that we may assist with?" Elizabeth deftly changed the subject, addressing Collins directly.

"Nothing that comes to mind right now," her brother-in-law answered. In the almost four months since taking over the living, Collins and his wife had become much-loved figures in Lambton and the surrounding area. Not only did the rector give interesting and educational sermons, but if there were any needs in the parish, great or small, Collins and Mary worked with their family to find a solution if they could not solve the issue on their own.

Mary was popular just by virtue of the fact that she was her Aunt Maddie's niece. Aunt Maddie was the daughter of the late John Worthington, who had held the living for well over thirty years and was well loved by all to this day.

"Are Charlotte and Mr. Wright riding to Meryton with us?" Jane asked.

"Yes, they are. It is well that both our brothers Collins and Wright have reliable curates, so they are able to leave their parishes," Elizabeth informed her sister. The former Miss Lucas had married Mr. Wright in early February. She was a part of the group of ex-Meryton residents very happily ensconced in the area.

As Richard sat watching his family banter back and forth, he reminded himself that there was one more promise to his late wife he had yet to fulfil. He would honour Anne's wishes and re-marry one he loved and have the family that he always wanted.

He remembered how intrigued he had been with the second-to-last Bennet daughter, Kitty, who was yet young. Since attending the art school in London she had asked to be called Catherine.

She had recently turned ten and eight, but with him close to thirty, would there be too much of an age difference? It would be moot unless she was interested in him as a man she could consider marrying. Richard resolved that he would not pre-judge anything for her; he would wait to see what their reactions were, one to the other, when he met her again.

There was one thing that he was quite sure of; he was not interested in any simpering misses of the Ton who would fawn over him and agree with every word out of his mouth, regardless how nonsensical. The same ladies who would not have given him any notice as Colonel Fitzwilliam would trip over one another to gain it from Viscount Smithtown. That is not to say that being a member of the first circles would disqualify a lady, but there were many other attributes that Richard desired in a wife. Affected beauty and style, and discussing the weather, were not two of them.

He was well aware how important it was for him to marry and sire a legitimate heir as his late brother had failed in that, as he had in so many areas of his life. During his period of mourning and knowing that he would soon need to make good on his promises to his Anne, each time he considered what he wanted in his life's mate a vision of Catherine Bennet found its way into his head.

A few days later, the group set off on the journey southward. As they had planned, on the second day of travel, Elizabeth and

William Darcy's vehicle made the turn toward London.

CHAPTER 15

A happy couple departed the home of the accoucheur, Mr. Ashcroft, as he had confirmed that Elizabeth was with child and that she should feel the quickening in about two months. Her confinement was projected to be in November or December.

Both the housekeeper and butler at Darcy House were surprised when the two arrived, as they had received no prior notice from the master and mistress. "Do not make yourselves uneasy," Elizabeth assured the Paytons. "Our coming was a spur of the moment decision as we had intended to go directly to Hertfordshire. We have instead determined to depart in the morning so as long as cook can make us a light dinner. Cold meats and cheese will suffice, and we will need no further assistance this evening."

With the housekeeper and butler relieved that they had not erred or missed a note from the master or mistress, the Darcys made their way to their suite, aware that they were without their personal servants as the two had carried on to Hertfordshire.

After the light meal that proved their cook's worth as she had been given such short notice, the couple shared a long, languid, steaming bath. It was the first time the couple joined in the bathtub and neither noticed, nor cared about, the amount of water than ended up outside of the tub.

Once they turned their attention to their surroundings and realised that the water had cooled significantly, the two dried each other off, then Darcy picked his wife up as if she weighed nothing and carried her to their bed. They had shared a bed since that first night he had made her his wife. Neither subscribed to the idea that the mistress and master should sleep in separate chambers, and both were gratified to learn they shared this belief in common.

Once she was on the bed, Darcy knelt next to her and reverently kissed her belly. There was no visible sign yet, but he could not stop himself kissing the place where their daughter or son was growing. "You were created out of love," he told his wife's belly, "and you will be surrounded by love all of your life, whether you are a son or daughter." Darcy's voice was thick with emotion.

"Our child's mother loves you with all of her being, William," Elizabeth whispered. He looked up and melted when he saw tears rolling down her cheeks, his words having overwhelmed her. Her eyes were filled with love and passion for him.

"My Lizzy," Darcy whispered as his mouth descended over hers. He ached to share with her the passion she fell into when she looked at him like that again. He would in turn share the depth of his own, knowing that both of them would be sleeping in the carriage again, as there was much to attend to before the sun came up.

--*-*-*-*-*-*-*-*-*-*-*

"Thank goodness you are both well!" Jane admonished her sister as the Darcys alighted from their carriage. "Where were you? We expected you yesterday evening."

"After our appointment, we decided it was too late to set out for Netherfield, so we spent the night at Darcy House and departed this morning. We considered sending a note, but we did not want to have a courier ride at night if it were not urgent, and we arrived not long after a rider would have this morning," Elizabeth explained.

"We sent a note to Longbourn last night to let Mama and Papa we had arrived safely, and we would *all* visit this morning,"

Jane informed her sister who had a look about her that she had not noticed before.

"We will wash and change, and will be ready within the hour," Elizabeth promised before Jane could ask any further questions.

After washing and changing, helped by their relieved personnel who were glad to see that the master and mistress were well, the two joined the rest of the family in the drawing room.

A relieved Georgiana hugged her brother and sister tightly. "We were well Giana; I am sorry we did not have a safe way to notify you we would arrive this morning," Darcy said as he kissed the top of his sister's head.

"Did I not say that Lizzy and her William were well?" Mary asked smugly. "Lizzy, what is it? You have a look about you; it is what I noticed on Mama when…Elizabeth Darcy are you with child?"

Elizabeth looked at her husband, who gave an almost imperceptible nod. "I am, and it was confirmed by Mr. Ashcroft yesterday. That was the reason we detoured to London. We were going to wait until after the quickening, but Mary is too perceptive!" Elizabeth gave her younger sister an accusing look. "Mary, do you or Jane have anything new to report yet?"

"Not I," Mary replied.

"Nor I," Jane reported.

"I suggest we not say anything to Mama until after her confinement. She does not need anything else to worry about right now," Elizabeth opined.

"When will I be an Aunt, Lizzy?" Georgiana asked happily.

"According to the accoucheur, November or December," Elizabeth smiled sweetly at her sister.

"Darcy is going to be a father!" the Viscount exclaimed. "Did you know about this, Aunt Cat?"

"I suspected, but I was sure that William and Lizzy would tell us when they felt the time was right. Richard, when will my brother and sister arrive from Town?" Lady Catherine deftly changed the subject.

"They will depart London a week before Parliament recesses for the summer," the Viscount informed his aunt.

With that, the Darcys led the way to carriages ready to convey them the three miles to Longbourn.

*_*_*_*_*_*_*_*_*_*_*_*_*_*

"Jane, Lizzy, Mary, it is so good to see you," Lydia said as she greeted them in the drive. She had returned from her school a few days earlier.

"I suppose we are superfluous," Collins indicated himself and his fellow brothers-in-law.

"I did not forget you, Brother Collins!" Lydia stated with a mild rebuke. "Is a girl not allowed to greet her sisters first? Welcome Aunt Cat; I am glad to see that you were not slighted that I did not greet you immediately." Lydia stated impertinently as she challenged her brother to make further comment.

"It is good to see you looking so happy, Lyddie," Jane hugged her youngest sister. "Where is Kitty?"

"If you mean *Catherine*, she is visiting Maria Lucas. Welcome, Lord Hilldale; I did not see you skulking behind everyone," Lydia teased.

"How many times have I asked that you call me Richard, *Miss* Lydia?" Richard grinned at the impertinent miss.

Lydia could still be lively at times, but it was the only residue left of who she was before. She always kept within the bounds of propriety now and the rude, brash girl was gone. The new Lydia was kind and considerate and was adept at thinking of others' needs before her own.

"In that case, welcome *Richard*! Mama is in the drawing room, and Papa is working in his study. We need to go and see her before Mama thinks that I am hiding you away." Lydia led the way to the drawing room.

"My sons and daughters," Fanny Bennet welcomed her family. "Giana, you are even more beautiful than when I last saw you!"

"I thank you, Aunt Fanny," Georgiana blushed. Though all residual effects from Ramsgate were long gone, she was still a shy girl.

"Welcome Cat; you look well. Please come sit next to me, for I want nothing to do with all that youthful energy," Fanny patted the seat next to her as she smiled at Lady Catherine. "Richard, were you hiding? I did not see you. Welcome."

Lydia made a poor attempt at hiding her laughter at her mother's comment and was not entirely successful, earning her the gimlet eye from Richard, who sent her a mock glare.

"Hello all," Catherine Bennet offered, letting everyone know she had returned from Lucas Lodge. When she noticed the Viscount looking at her, she blushed becomingly. Not only had the former Kitty matured in the last months, but she had grown even more lovely than Richard remembered.

For the first time, Fanny Bennet looked at her second daughter. "Lizzy, you are with child!" It was a statement, not a question.

"How did you know, Mama?" an amazed Elizabeth asked.

"I have always been able to spot a lady with child. Do you think I would miss the same in my own daughter?" Fanny asked, her brow arched in question proving that it was Elizabeth who was mistaken.

"I suppose not," Elizabeth laughed. "My state has been confirmed and I will enter my confinement November or December."

"What did you just say?" Bennet asked as he joined the family in the drawing room. "Will I be a father and grandfather in the same year? At least the new aunt or uncle will be older than your child!"

"It will be amusing that our children will be almost the same age," Elizabeth smiled up at him.

"Come, my dear, it is time for your rest." Bennet helped his wife to stand then guided her up the stairs.

When Bennet returned, he approached Lady Catherine. "Cat, Fanny has a request. She would like to know if you will agree to be our guest at Longbourn, for she finds your company calming. I, of course, would appreciate your presence as well, as you are both family and friend."

"It would be my pleasure to remain here with my friend, Thomas. As long as one my nephews agrees to have my maid pack for me and then to transport both her and my trunk for me," Lady Catherine replied.

"I will gladly take care of that for you, Aunt Cat," Richard volunteered. He was grateful to have an excuse to visit Longbourn again so he would be in the company of Catherine Bennet.

--*-*-*-*-*-*-*-*-*-*-*-*

A few nights later, a dinner was hosted at Longbourn. Lady Catherine was acting as hostess given that her friend was so close to her confinement it would be too much of an exertion. In addition to the residents of Netherfield, Philips, Lucas, Wright, Long, and Goulding families were invited, and all had accepted.

Fanny Bennet well knew what the pains starting in her lower back portended, but she ignored them, intent on enjoying the evening after the pleasant dinner party. As the pains increased in intensity and frequency, they became harder to hide.

"Fanny, I am about to put my foot down and carry you above stairs myself. What say you to letting your husband feel of use to take you?" Lady Catherine leaned over and asked her friend quietly. Fanny laughed, which caused her to audibly gasp, and Bennet shot up to assist.

"Jane, ask Bingley to ride to Mrs. Perkins and have her come to Longbourn, then request the same of Mr. Jones," Bennet asked softly. Jane's eyes grew large as she understood what was happening as she saw Lady Catherine assisting her uncomfortable looking mother from the dining parlour. By the time she leaned toward her husband and conveyed her father's request, there were none who were unaware that something was afoot.

"The babe is coming tonight!" Bingley blurted out as he stood and made for the stables.

"As you all heard, it seems that Fanny and I are to be parents again. The newest Bennet has decided to join our auspicious company. You have my sincere regrets for ending the evening prematurely," Bennet announced to the wide-eyed diners, who laughed with him. It was Lady Lucas who took over and started directing the staff to clean up in the home of her lifelong friend, waving off Bennet's appreciation and telling him that he was to go have a drink as all men must learn to do when their job is to wait patiently.

As the last guest departed, Bingley rode up to the house and vaulted off his horse. "Mr. Jones will be here momentarily, and Mrs. Perkins was making her cart ready when I departed her cottage," Bingley reported to his father-in-law when he strode into the drawing room. Other than Jane and Elizabeth, who were assisting Lady Catherine, the rest of the family were present.

Mr. Jones arrived within five minutes of Bingley's return, and Mrs. Perkins a quarter hour after him. Both went directly to the birthing chamber, as they were familiar with its location. Bennet chuckled when she arched a brow at him as she was about to deliver his sixth child. She was one of the few, besides himself, who could calm his Fanny down regardless of how upset she was.

Mrs. Perkins took charge as soon as she arrived, shooing Mr. Jones out while telling him that he would be summoned if needed, then she herself examined Fanny. "You could have done this without me. Now I see a 'ead! Bear down, Fanny. NOW!" she commanded. Moments later the chamber was filled with the plaintive wails of a new-born babe.

"My, our brother is loud, Mama!" Elizabeth exclaimed as she cleaned him so he could be handed to their mother.

"Did you say brother, Lizzy?" Fanny asked in genuine surprise, not believing her ears.

"Yes, Mama, that is exactly what I said!" Elizabeth confirmed. As if to highlight that he was a boy, the newest Bennet sent a stream of urine into the air before Jane managed to secure his napkin.

"You son is on the small side, Fanny, but he looks hale and heathy to me," Lady Catherine assured her friend.

"Mrs. Perkins, I am having the same pains again!" Fanny panicked.

"Yes, well, I figured we'd get to that sooner or later. Push again, Fanny, as hard as you can," the midwife instructed. Ten minutes later a second wail joined the first.

"Another boy, Fanny! You have twin sons," Lady Catherine laughed as she held the heir while Jane cleaned the second one and Elizabeth helped with her mother.

"How will I tell them apart?" Fanny asked tiredly as the midwife massaged her belly to help expel the afterbirth.

"They are not identical, Mama. The older has my colouring and his brother has Jane's. They both have blue eyes like their oldest sister," Elizabeth told her mother. "Do you have any names picked out yet, Mama?"

"We did not pick a name as we did not know what the babe's gender would be. As much as we hoped for a boy, after five daughters we did not want to assume," Fanny smiled ruefully when Elizabeth and Jane lowered their brothers into the waiting arms of their mother. "You had blue eyes at birth as well, Lizzy. By the time you were half a year old, they turned the colour they are now."

"I will go and ask Thomas to join you, Fanny," Lady Catherine volunteered.

"Lizzy and I will join you, Aunt Cat," Jane added. "It will give our parents some time alone with our brothers."

--*-*-*-*-*-*-*-*-*-*-*-*-*

Despite having done this five times before, Bennet had been pacing in the drawing room. No matter how much anyone, including his sister-in-law, tried to calm him, he could not as his Fanny was older and there were ever more concerns as one grew older. Birthing children was for the young, not the middle-aged. He was most worried because as he had heard almost no screaming, and for all the other births his house had shook with them. His heart was racing and stopping in turns as he counted the seconds of silence. He was about to run up the stairs when the drawing room door opened to reveal Lady Catherine, followed by his two oldest daughters. All three were smiling and laughing. He took some encouragement from those signs but braced himself for their news.

"Go see your wife and sons, Thomas. They are waiting for you," Lady Catherine announced.

Bennet started towards the door and then he stopped dead in his tracks. "Did you say *sons*, Cat?"

"Yes, Papa, you have *two* sons," Jane's smile brightened at the sharing of the news, and without another word Bennet bounded up the stairs as if he were a young man again.

Collins led those congratulating the Bennet sisters on the birth of their brothers. He had married the woman he loved and was exceedingly happy to be ministering to Lambton's parishioners. Given the annual value of the living, he wanted for nothing. As it was, he and Mary were able to save well over seventy percent of their earnings. Perhaps their son would be able to purchase a small estate, were they to be so blessed.

--*-*-*-*-*-*-*-*-*-*-*-*

Bennet marvelled as he looked on his wife and sons. He picked up his heir, who was sleeping after nourishing himself from his mother. "What about names, Thomas?" Fanny asked.

"How would you feel if we were to name one after my father and one after yours, Fanny?" Bennet asked.

"That is a fine idea, but your heir should bear your father's name," Fanny insisted.

"It is settled then. This young man will be Adam, and that scamp in your arms Elias. What of middle names, Fanny?" Bennet asked.

"I would like both to have their father's name; may we use Tom?" Fanny suggested.

"In that case we have Adam Tom Bennet and Elias Tom Bennet," Bennet stated proudly. "May I take them to meet their sisters, brothers, and the rest of the family?" Bennet asked, knowing his wife needed to sleep and wanting to give her the chance.

Mrs. Hill held little Elias as she followed the master down to the drawing room where he proudly introduced the newest Bennets to those present.

--*-*-*-*-*-*-*-*-*-*-*-*

A sennight later Darcy and Elizabeth took an early morning walk that led them to Oakham Mount. They were discussing the cause for them being able to sneak out for an hour or two as after four days abed to recover from the effort of birthing twins, Fanny Bennet was doing much better. She moved slowly, but she was out of bed and well on her way to recovery.

Everyone had supported Bennet in his insistence that a wet-nurse be hired for night-time feedings. Fanny tried to insist that she was capable of managing both of her sons' feedings, but after the first night of interrupted sleep, she had appreciated the wisdom of her husband's plan.

It had not escaped anyone's notice that Catherine Bennet

and Richard seemed to find whatever time they could to be in one another's company. With Lydia and Giana having bonded as lifelong friends, Mrs. Annesley was able to act as chaperone for the Viscount and Miss Bennet.

The Gardiners had arrived the day after the birth and stayed for four days before returning to London. The Gardiner children were fascinated by their baby twin cousins, while their father and mother were happy that their sister had survived the birth.

When the two Darcys arrived at the summit of the hill, they held each other tightly as the sun rose over the fields of Hertfordshire. As the sun lighted her face, Darcy kissed his wife, pouring his heart and soul into it; she returned the gift. When they pulled apart, Elizabeth looked out at the view and smiled when she spotted Lucas Lodge. "What amuses you my dearest, loveliest Elizabeth?" Darcy asked, hoping to share it with her.

"Lucas Lodge," Elizabeth pointed. "Would we have found each other had you not kissed me and then left the area? As much as I railed against it, *the kiss at Lucas Lodge* was the absolute best thing that could have happened to me."

"Did I do a creditable job wooing my Bennet girl?" Darcy asked, giving his wife one of his dimple-revealing smiles.

"You most certainly did, William, you most certainly did!"

EPILOGUE

Pemberley, ten years later, early summer

"Mama! Adam and Elias are ordering me around again!" nine-year-old Ben Darcy complained to his mother, who was sitting on the terrace with Lady Catherine.

"We are your uncles!" Adam spoke for the twins, who were ten.

"Have we not spoken to you about this, Adam and Elias?" Lady Catherine demanded while trying to keep a straight face.

"Yes mother," both boys chorused as they kicked the dirt while Ben looked on feeling very smug.

"What have we told you about tattling, Ben?" Elizabeth asked, instantly wiping the smug look from her son's face.

Ben Darcy had three siblings: Tiffany, eight, who to the delight of her father was the image of her mother, both in looks and character; Fanny, who was five and looked very much like her beloved Aunty Giana; and the baby Tom, who was just one.

Three years after the birth of her twins, Fanny Bennet had succumbed to a bad case of influenza that developed into pneumonia. Less than two years later, Thomas Bennet married Lady Catherine de Bourgh, his and his wife's best friend. When she became Lady Catherine Bennet, she did not repine the loss of the de Bourgh name.

Bennet, his wife, and their sons lived at Longbourn for four to five months each year, then spent the rest of the time with their daughters either in Town or at one of their estates. For some reason, which he claimed had nothing to do with the library, Bennet had an affinity for Pemberley.

There was hardly a day that went by that Lady Catherine did not think about her daughter, now gone for more than ten years, or her brother who had passed the same year as Fanny from a similar malady.

Eighteen months before his death, Lord Matlock witnessed his son and heir marry the almost twenty-year-old Miss Catherine Bennet. The new viscountess had been with child when the Earl had passed away. The new Earl and Countess named their firstborn, now six, Reginald Thomas Fitzwilliam. In subsequent years, they had added a daughter and a son, and Catherine was with child again.

Lydia had insisted on remaining at the Wrightfield School for Young Ladies for two full years, then had requested and completed a year of finishing school. She had only come out at twenty, after mourning her mother for a year. Her experience with the long-dead George Wickham made her very wary of men until she met the Marquess of Chatsworth, Henry Granville. After a year of courting and two proposals, Lydia accepted Mark's third. They have a son, Henry junior, who was not yet a year old.

After the rector who held the Longbourn and Meryton livings passed away, they were offered to Mr. Wright, who accepted with the support of his wife and four children. The Wrights were contented living at Longbourn parsonage, which was within easy distance of the Lucases. I would be remiss if I did not note here that the new Mrs. Bennet never once tried to tell the rector how to write a sermon.

When Mr. Wright resigned, Darcy offered the two additional livings to William Collins, who was loved and respected in Lambton. With the additional two livings, his income increased to over two thousand per annum, most of which he and his frugal wife saved for the future as they had a son and two daughters. The family moved into the parsonage at Pemberley, the largest of the three, and were but a short walk away from their family.

The Bingleys were as happy as any couple could be and were as content at Ashford Dale as they were in town when they chose to visit it. They had three daughters before they were blessed with a son named Charles Junior, called Charlie. Charlie was two now, and Jane was once again with child.

The Hursts had finally had their first child five years earlier, and to the relief of Hurst and his father the child was a boy. Less than two years later, as sometimes happens, he was followed by a girl, a little brother, and finally little Caroline was born. They named her Caroline in memory and honour of Louisa and Charles's mother. The *other* Caroline was never mentioned by any who had known her.

The Hursts generally visited both the Bingley and Darcy estates at least once a year. Their time at Ashford Dale was especially enjoyable as, two years after taking possession of the estate, Bingley had brought his Aunt Hildebrand to live with him and Jane. As the keeper of Bingley history, the children always clamoured to hear her tales.

Lady Elaine, the Dowager Countess of Matlock, was happy in the dower house at the Matlock estate. She would always miss her Reggie, but she was surrounded by her grandchildren, her own and the Darcys'; she, like her former sister-in-law, was a surrogate grandmother to the Darcy grandchildren and the three children of Georgiana and Brandon Welles.

Giana had met Brandon during her second season when she was ten and nine and he five and twenty. He owned Bliss Hill in Staffordshire, only thirty miles from Pemberley. After a combined six-month courtship and betrothal period passed, the couple, very much in love, had married at Pemberley. Lydia Bennet stood up for her sister and best friend. Lydia and Giana were best of friends and often visited one another. Giana's daughter

Anne was born a year after Giana's wedding, followed by a son a little more than two years later; then there was another daughter, now almost two.

The three boys, as the rest of the older Darcy children, were excited because later that day all of the family would arrive, bringing with them a horde of cousins to Pemberley, or in the twins' case nephews and nieces. It was the Darcys' turn to host the family for two months of the summer. As soon as the first carriage was sighted, one which had the Matlock crest on the door, Ben, Adam, and Elias forgot their petty disagreements and charged toward the courtyard to greet the Fitzwilliams.

Darcy walked up behind his wife and wound his arms around her belly. He and Elizabeth looked on with pleasure from the terrace, which gave them a full view of the front of the house. She leaned into him, smiling in welcome as she looked up and met his eyes.

The love story which began with a kiss at Lucas Lodge would be told each successive generation of Darcys, and each retelling ended with the reminder that Elizabeth and William Darcy were happily married for well over sixty years.

The End

BOOKS BY THIS AUTHOR

The Kiss At Lucas Lodge

As he does in canon, Fitzwilliam Darcy slights Elizabeth Bennet at the assembly in Meryton. The militia arrive in Meryton earlier than in Miss Austin's work with the seducer Wickham already a member of the unit. Jane Bennet is invited to Netherfield and does get ill, but not as severely ill as in canon.

Wickham spins his pack of lies and after being slighted by the man she now detests; Elizabeth believes them without question. That is the point that this story leaves canon behind. The Wickham in this tale is even more despicable than he is in canon.

What happens when Elizabeth refuses to dance with Darcy at Lucas Lodge, as she cannot abide to be around the proud man, he kisses her? What do her family and the neighbours say? How do Miss Bingley, Lady Catherine, and the Matlocks react? Does Wickham try to interfere? How does Elizabeth react, as she disdains the man greatly?

Will Darcy ever be able to redeem himself in Elizabeth's eyes?